What's Tuesday?

BOOKS BY MITZI DALE

Bryna Means Courage
On My Own
The Sky's the Limit
Round the Bend

Mitzi Dale

What's Tuesday?

A Groundwood Book ✶ Douglas & McIntyre

Toronto Vancouver

Groundwood Books / Douglas & McIntyre Ltd.
585 Bloor Street West
Toronto, Ontario M6G 1K5

Canadian Cataloguing in Publication Data
Dale, Mitzi
What's Tuesday?
"A Groundwood book".
ISBN 0-88899-281-5
I. Title.
PS8557.A453W42 1997   jC813'.54   C97-930050-9
PZ7.D34Wh 1997

Cover illustration by Alan Barnard
Design by Michael Solomon
Printed and bound in Canada by Webcom

To Patsy, Shelley and
everyone at Groundwood

ONE

"Now I get it," Gramps said. Then he fell forward, face first into his soup.

We were having my mum's famous green pea soup that evening—a purée of dried split peas and potatoes—and as it's rather thick, it didn't splatter wildly in all directions. My brother and I sat on each side of my gramps and I noticed we both took a simultaneous and gentle swipe at our cheeks with our sleeves. Nobody looked at anybody else.

"Gary," my mum finally said. "Your father's dead."

"Yes," my dad said. He was looking at his dad.

I remember thinking, "I'm glad I haven't fought with Gramps for awhile," because he'd been living with us for nearly a year by that time, and we'd had a few doozies. When he first moved in with his nosy questions I just went to my room and stewed for a couple of hours, but my mum said to me, "Your grandfather's not made of china, Steph," so the next time he asked if all my girlfriends wore that much makeup to school, instead of saying, "This isn't much," or stomping off to my room or whatever, I just looked him in the eye and said, "Yes, they do."

Now my dad's dad, who had very little expression in his eyes or eyebrows, could do everything he needed to with his lips. Sometimes they were pressed together in two flat lines. Sometimes they were pursed out like a pucker—only he had no intention of kissing—and the lines around his lips came together like the spokes of a wheel. This time they pressed together and his chin jutted out in such a way as to create an inverted U. I've tried it in the mirror and it almost hurts.

Anyway, this is what I was thinking when Gramps did his face-plant, and I now know everyone else had their own thoughts. Matt was wondering if Gramps might be still alive and inhaling soup. Drowning in soup. Mum was wondering how all of the rest of us were. Were Matt and I scared? Was Dad going to cry or faint or go into shock? He did none of these, but it turns out that last line of Gramps'—"Now I get it"—had lodged in Dad's head and wouldn't leave.

It was in there when he said, "Elly, phone the doctor, will you?" It was in there when he went over to his dad and placed two fingers on his neck, then shook his head. It was in there when he asked Matt to get a pillow and me to get a dampened facecloth. We all carried out our duties just as he'd directed us to, and practically as soon as Gramps' face was wiped and his head was resting on a pillow instead of in the bowl of soup, there was a knock at the door.

Dr. Brewster, who was even younger than my dad and who had only seen Gramps once in his life, came in and listened to his stopped heart and said what we all already knew.

"He's dead."

Then he asked if my grandfather had made any arrangements, which he had, and he and my dad lifted him onto the carpet and stretched him out so that when the undertakers came to get him he wouldn't have stiffened into a bent position. Again my dad put the pillow under his head, which struck me as weird at the time but it did look better.

The doctor didn't know any of us—Mum and I go to the woman half of a doctor couple and Dad and Matt go to the male half—so he didn't hang around much after he'd mumbled a bit about how quick it would have been and how much he liked Gramps even from that one visit. I wondered if Gramps had told the doctor what he'd told us: that he wanted a young one so that he'd be fresh and up on all the latest tricks. Soon a couple of guys wearing suits and keeping their heads down came and took Gramps away on a stretcher.

This event changed our lives, though, at first, not drastically. We all went about our daily routines pretty much as we always had, but each one of us had a new awareness. It was like really seeing how you live for the first time. It was like being an alien and getting to inhabit the body of an average Canadian in the late twentieth century.

It was weird.

TWO

It was a little over a week after Gramps died that I had my headshift, as I like to call it. My brother called his a switcheroo, my dad called his a revelation, and my mum said hers was an epiphany. The last two are just a bit too religious-sounding for my taste and switcheroo, though excellent, too comic-booky. Headshift it is.

I had my headshift during Current Events. It came as such a powerful idea, such a different way of looking at things, that I would never in a million years have connected it to the events of the week before: my Gramps' death and burial. I mean, everything had gone so smoothly, you'd have thought we were dead-grandfather specialists. The actual event I have already related, and it happened on a Friday night. Gramps had been so meticulous about his "arrangements" that we had nothing to do but make sure our most solemn clothes were clean—which they were as they were so seldom worn—and show up at the funeral home on Sunday.

Gramps had written his instructions to the letter. He was to be buried in the simplest and cheapest casket and there was to be no service, just a gathering of immediate family and his oldest and dearest friends. Well, his oldest and dearest friends were all dead, so the four of us drove into the city to the funeral home.

This was not my first funeral, but it was Matt's. I had gone to my aunt's years ago when I was eight and, even though my mum had prepared me, was quite surprised to see the top part of the coffin flipped open and my aunt's slack face inside. Gramps, thank heaven, had specified a closed-casket funeral. I've asked what the point of an open one is and they say it's so you can really believe that the beloved dead one is actually dead. Well, since we'd all seen him go, we had no trouble believing that, but it occurred to me that Gramps couldn't have known he was going to kick it in front of the four of us so...why did he specify that the casket be closed? It couldn't have been vanity—he would never have done all those manoeuvres with his lips if he'd been vain. I concluded that it was all part of his personally stark style.

Gramps didn't like to waste time. No service about "returning to his Lord" or "ashes to ashes" and all that stuff, and no gawking at the dead person, which was also a waste of time. He used to say to me when I was flopped on the couch reading a magazine, "You'll never get this hour back again, you know." In fact my dad was surprised Gramps lived as long as he did after retirement—which he took later than most people—because he thought the second my grandfather considered himself unuseful, he'd decide living was a waste of time. I don't know.

Anyway, we stood around for a bit in the small room that seemed quite large with just the four of us in it and looked at the simple casket he had pre-ordered. I didn't actually touch it, but it seemed to be covered in flocked paper—not red flocking on a gold background or anything like that, just an all-over flocking in a subdued blue-grey. Some men carried the coffin out to a hearse and we followed it to the cemetery. There was absolutely no need to put our lights on and stop traffic because there was just us and the hearse ahead. We didn't even stay around to watch it being lowered into its spot beside my grandmother, who had died before I could remember her.

I watched my dad's face to see if the headstone with his mum's name on it would make him sad, but he wasn't even looking at it. He seemed far, far away. Matt and I both noticed, though, that beneath my grandmother's name was our gramps' name and birth date already carved. The space for the year of his death was blank. Just think, his tombstone had been waiting for him like that for thirteen years. He had planned so far ahead that when my grandmother died he'd gone ahead and had them put him on there, too.

Even though my gramps had stipulated that the mourners were to go to a particular hotel and have sandwiches and tea, as there were only the four of us, we didn't do that. I suppose that must have messed up someone's accounts somewhere as this whole funeral had been not only pre-arranged but pre-paid, but we just didn't feel like following through on that one. I realize now that this was setting the tone for our future adventures, but at the time it seemed a pretty modest, almost unnoticeable infraction.

We went, instead, to a fast-food place and sat there in our solemn clothes and carried on as if we hadn't just buried Gramps. We talked about the coming week and who needed what washed and ironed and who was going to cook dinner and who was going to clean the garage. Mum said she was tired of having to scrub the bathtub *before* she had a bath. Dad said he'd like it on my night to cook if we could have something other than spaghetti. Matt said he needed money for a school trip. We all behaved just the same.

But we were all different.

THREE

So I'm sitting in Current Events and Mrs. Di Bartolo is spreading out the front pages of various national and local papers. She is making the point, which she never tires of, that different newspapers treat different items of news differently. She uses the phrase "manipulating our awareness" a lot. It's Tuesday. This happens to be the day that our local rag—the *Leader-Bulletin*—comes out and I get to read what Andy Stemming's mum, who writes a weekly column, thinks of the five Hollywood movies I get to choose from tonight when it's cheap. This, however, is not front-page news, and it is the front pages that really grab Mrs. Di Bartolo. The national newspaper has big black headlines: THE ECONOMY. The *Leader-Bulletin* has a picture of the president of the Rotary, Sue Wassman's dad, shaking hands with some kid I don't recognize from another school who's going to France for a year on exchange.

Now my dad always says the purpose of a local paper is to get everyone's picture in it who lives in the town. Sue Wassman's dad gets in there more than most, but it's true that my mum's been in. She was one of the people they stopped on the street once and asked: "What do you think of the new parking meters?" The new parking meters on the main street don't have slots for nickels and dimes anymore, just quarters and loonies. There's a head-and-shoulders picture of my mum with the words: "I just park on a side street and walk the block and a half now—it's good exercise."

Anyway, it certainly counts as "being in the newspaper."

My brother has had his photo in quite a bit. When he was into soccer he was right there with his team in their Hindle's Hardware uniforms. Then his Dolly's Donuts baseball uniform and, more recently, he made it in as an example of terrifying youth on skateboards and rollerblades *on our main streets!* My dad and I haven't made it in yet, but we feel the family has been well represented.

Once I offered my dad's opinion about the purpose of local newspapers to Mrs. Di Bartolo and she said, "Mm," and moved on to the point she really wanted to make. Mrs. Di Bartolo is one of those nice teachers who doesn't want to inhibit you by saying you're wrong. She feels that with Current Events and all that manipulation of awareness going on out there, *any* answer is valid because it's what the journalist or photographer evokes in *you*. This is probably why she didn't clue in immediately to the tremendous power of the headshift I was experiencing in her class that day.

It's Tuesday. Tuesday. What is Tuesday?

All of a sudden the concept of a Tuesday—or a Monday or a Friday for that matter—made no sense to me. I mean, why name this day Tuesday? Why name this day at all? This particular day was never going to come around again. This particular day was unique. If it had any name at all it should be Day Gazillion and Four, say. But why count the days? And would you start counting from the first man or woman or would you start counting from the first swirling of gases?

Now, unfortunately, Mrs. Di Bartolo asked me a question when I was at this point in my thoughts and I had no idea what she was expecting of me, so I said, "Why Tuesday?"

"Mm," she said. "Yes. Well, the *Leader-Bulletin* comes out on Tuesday, of course."

Poor Mrs. Di Bartolo. She was trying to cover for me.

"No, I mean, why do we call this day Tuesday?"

"Because it's Tuesday, idiot."

That was from Laurie Hicks, not Mrs. Di Bartolo. Laurie and I often squared off in Current Events, taking different sides of issues. It was fun and it passed the time.

When the class had stopped laughing I asked, "How do you know?"

"I know because yesterday was Monday and tomorrow is Wednesday." More laughter from the class. "And I know," Laurie said, going up to Mrs. Di Bartolo's desk and taking the *Leader-Bulletin*, "because it says so right here." She was pointing to the top right-hand portion of the newspaper where the date was printed.

Everybody laughed at that, even Mrs. Di Bartolo. Laurie had a dramatic style, which I appreciated, but I was able to remain very quiet until I had people's attention—something Laurie wasn't able to do. She always grabbed for the attention.

"Do you believe everything you read in print?" I asked.

The whole class went "ooh" because Mrs. Di Bartolo spent so much time on not believing everything we read in print. Laurie seemed to think it was a cheap point instead of a very good one. She sneered.

"That says Tuesday," I said, "because we have all for years agreed on Tuesday. But what if we called it Blundfuggle?"

The class exploded.

"Mm, yes." Mrs. Di Bartolo tried getting back to her lesson. "Or we could call it martedi or mardi—"

"No, Mrs. Di Bartolo," I said. "That's not my point."

"What *is* your point?" Laurie asked, leaving her mouth hanging open.

"My point is: Tuesday doesn't really exist."

"So we're not here."

"We're here, but Tuesday isn't."

Andy Stemming jumped up then with his books. "If Tuesday isn't here, Mrs. D., can I go now?"

Mrs. Di Bartolo smiled and made a little waving motion at Andy in particular to sit down and at the class in general to settle down.

"Perhaps Stephanie and Laurie will continue their philosophical discussion some other time. This Tuesday—*today*—I would like to discuss the manipulation of our awareness by—"

I wasn't listening.

Why were they all so convinced of Tuesday? Why should we go through seven days and then start over again? Did the trees know that? Did the trees swaying in the wind think, "Oh, good, it's Tuesday again." Or did the trees just keep going? Day after day after day.

Days I can understand. The sun rises, the sun sets, and it starts again—but it's a different *day*.

The seasons I can understand. The sun gets lower in the sky, the snow flies. But weeks? The weeks don't really start again. It's a hoax! Someone invented weeks to keep us fooled. Someone called a day Tuesday and convinced us that when the sun rose and set seven more times we'd be at Tuesday again! It makes no sense! We're not at Tuesday again, we're

19

on to something entirely new...seven sunrises later. And nobody saw it. They thought that because on the day named Tuesday they got up and went to Current Events and finished their day at the Tuesday night movie, then did it all again seven days later, that it really *was* Tuesday!

Why did we all put up with this? Billions of us.

"See ya next Blundfuggle," Laurie sneered as we drifted out of Mrs. Di Bartolo's class. But something told me, even then, that I wouldn't necessarily always make every Blundfuggle a repeat of the last. Not at all.

FOUR

Dinner that night was weird. Gramps had been dead a week and a half now and my dad had once again taken over the chair that he'd had before Gramps came to live with us. So he and my mum sat opposite each other, and Matt and I sat across from each other. We were all very quiet, quieter than we had been during dinner for the whole past week. My mum liked us to eat dinner together because, she said, it was one of the few times we got to relax together as a family since everyone was so busy. I think by "everyone," she meant me and Matt. And by "relaxed," she meant sitting down.

Anyway, there we were sitting down to Tuesday's dinner. (This is no joke. My mum and dad shopped twice a month, together, then made up a list of menus for the next two weeks, putting "Matt dinner" and "Steph dinner" in the Wednesday and Thursday slots.) Tuesday was always a casserole or stir-fry made from the leftovers of whatever mound of meat we ate on Sunday, in this case turkey. Monday was always a complete break from whatever meat was eaten on Sunday so that it would "come up fresh" on Tuesday. If there should happen to be leftovers of the leftovers, these were wrapped and labelled and frozen and any one of the four of us could take them to work or to school and nuke them, although only Mum and Dad ever did this.

"I've never done anything crazy in my life," my dad said.

Mum and Matt and I looked up at him from our chunks of creamed turkey over rice. There was a long silence.

"You married Mum," Matt said.

"You had us," I added, though both of us knew this was just one of those gap fillers. All of their friends had had two kids, too, and most of them had managed a boy and a girl. How did they do that?

My dad had never looked more put upon to me than he did at that moment. Mum was looking at him across the table. She nodded, slowly, as if she was really listening, not to just acknowledge him so she could get in what she wanted to say.

"I wouldn't know how," he said.

Again my mum nodded, and again Matt and I experienced that powerful urge to fill the gap.

"You could grow a beard," Matt said.

Instead of kicking him under the table, which would only get him going even worse, I reached over with my foot and pressed it slowly on top of his, simultaneously boring into him with A Look.

My friends' parents had always remarked on my

own parents' ability to handle the stresses of life with advance planning and a minimum of fuss, though I didn't really notice this until I was about twelve.

I'd spent the night at Lisa Farrow's house. Her dad had forgotten to pick up a video for us. Her mum had forgotten to get in the requisite chips and pop, and so Lisa was handed a mittful of bills and we walked to a convenience store ourselves and paid twice as much for everything. The paper boy came to collect and there was no little envelope with his name on it tucked behind the phone near the door. And there was no jar with small bills in it in the kitchen—petty cash we called it at my house—that we could dig into either, so we had to pay him out of the leftover mittful.

Then, the next morning, when Lisa's mum had completely forgotten that she'd said she could drive me home and she was already late for some meeting in the exact opposite direction of my house and I said that was okay my mum could pick me up on the way back from Matt's soccer practice, she turned to me while she was buttoning up her coat and grabbing her shoulder bag and said, "Your mum's so organized!" Then she smoothed her hair and pinched her cheeks, and as she drove away she was using the rearview mirror of the car to apply her lipstick.

Other mothers began to look exotic to me then.

They were always rushing around. They sometimes seemed to have been crying. They seemed to be always flustered or enraged or giggly but never in that calm, "Here's what we're going to do and here's how I propose we do it" state. They carried unnecessary things in their purses and blew a week's pay on shoes. They were *emotional.* So just at that point in life when I'd come to the realization that my mother was terribly defective in some way, just when I'd decided that everything the other parents admired about her was what was in fact wrong with her—the trouble with *you,* Mum, is—I felt the return pressure of Matt's foot up against my foot and he was tilting his head a little and giving me A Look back.

Mum was crying. Not sobbing or heaving her shoulders or anything, but as Dad sat there looking across at her, big wet tears were rolling down either side of her nose.

How can you say the trouble with *you* is when someone's sitting there doing the very thing you thought they couldn't do?

Go have parents.

FIVE

"Before we do anything crazy," my mother said, wiping at the tears that weren't stopping, "I just want to say that the kids don't have to come along."

I can't tell you what that sentence did to me. I felt prickly all through my body, especially my legs. Matt told me later he felt like he'd just swallowed a wad of dry bread that had stuck in his gullet.

"Come along," so clearly implied "going away," that we both reacted to it physically even without analyzing it at all. If Mum had said, "go along," it wouldn't have had the same effect, because you can "go along" with a plan to paint the house purple or "go along" with a decision to move into an apartment downtown and use public transport instead of two cars. Each of these options was nothing compared to what they ended up doing.

"I've read," she said, wiping away, "that anything parents do after the kids are ten years old is *their* adventure, not the kids'. It wouldn't be fair."

Who would I live with? Lisa? I mean, her mum was pretty and giddy and exotic but...she'd drive me *insane* full time. Laurie? I liked our verbal sparring two or three times a week, but...every day? I could just imagine the dinnertime conversation. It would be like the Debating Society From Hell.

"Where exactly did you read that, Mum?" Matt asked.

It broke the tension.

Everybody started pouring out their hearts. My dad said that Canada was the number one nation people wanted to live in—according to a United Nations survey he'd read. So here we were in the number one nation, in a number one town, in a number one house. Why was everyone so...so...

He couldn't find a word for whatever it was everyone was.

"Blechh?" Matt said. A comic-book word.

"Blechh," my mum said. "Today I went to the bank as usual and the receptionist said, 'How are you' as usual and I said, 'Not bad' as usual. Not bad? I've got a wonderful husband, two great kids, a house, two cars, we're all healthy, and all I can say is 'Not bad'? But that's how I felt. Not great. Not happy. Just not bad. Blechh."

I told about my headshift and Matt told about his switcheroo.

"I thought it was just me," Dad said. "I thought I was having a mid-life crisis. I was paying bills and it suddenly hit me how much insurance we have. The house, the contents, the cars, dental, medical, on and on...and so much life insurance! It's like I'm betting I'm going to die."

"Blechh," Matt said.

"What if I were to bet on living?"

Then all the crazy ideas started coming out. We'd cash in our chips and live on a houseboat for a year. We'd go to Australia and live in the outback. We'd go to Mexico and bake in the sun like sleepy iguanas. We were the Swiss Family Robinson. Or better yet, a close-knit bunch of officers on Star Trek boldly going where no one had gone before. We wouldn't be sad or lonely drifters because we'd have each other.

That was the plan, anyway.

SIX

It happened fast. My parents each gave a month's notice at their jobs the very day after the teary dinner. My dad was purchasing agent for a company that manufactured brick. Not the small red and grey bricks like they use in houses, but the kind of brick that's used to build huge ovens or kilns in steel mills and stuff. So it was his job to know when they were going to manufacture what product and to see to it that the ingredients they needed for everything were right on the spot when they needed them. Some of the stuff came up from the States in trains and sometimes there were strikes going on and things like that. It was only after he'd left his job that I realized how much he was bothered by it. He worried about price hikes, customs clearance and stuff he called "office politics."

My mother said the office politics was the best part of her job. She called it "schmooze"—finding out who was dating whom and who was going to get transferred where. My mum worked in a bank, which was probably why she handled all the money on our adventure.

The FOR SALE sign was on the lawn the next

day, and because when the real estate agent asked my folks, "Do you wanna list or do you wanna sell?" and they said, "Sell," it was listed for a lot less than the almost identical house next door. My mum had read that if something wonderful is cooking when a house is shown it works on people subliminally, so each time potential buyers came through, she put an apple studded with cloves in the oven. Even amidst a whirlwind of discombobulation my parents still did things right. So the third couple to wander through the place bought it.

Once the house was sold we had sixty days to clear everything out, including ourselves. Sixty days. The countdown. In kindergarten and grade one the teachers used to whip us into a frenzy about Christmas by saying, "Just thirty more sleeps till Santa comes." Well, just sixty more sleeps and we would be out of there. Out of the house that Matt had lived in most of his life. Out of the house where I'd spent my "formative years." It was odd enough coming home from school and seeing FOR SALE; odder still to see the bright red and black SOLD sticker stretched diagonally across the sign.

The cars went first, both to guys in their early twenties who would actually work on them. The body on my mum's car was more patches of brown rust-proof paint than the original teal, but it was in excellent shape under the hood. My dad's car, on the other hand, looked okay outside but he was the kind of guy who never changed his oil, just kept topping it up, so the guy who got his would have to do a little engine work. Apparently, the insurance for the cars alone was thirty-two hundred dollars. We could each have a bus pass for eight years with that money!

When there were just thirty more sleeps to go, we had a garage sale. I went through my room three times, but by the end of the third survey I was able to give up stuff that I'd put in the can't-live-without-pile on the first. Things in the can't-live-without-pile were to go into storage. But when I saw that Matt had put his comics out on the lawn in boxes, I ran back upstairs and got my frog collection. I included everything: stuffed frogs, frog paper-weights and froggie banks, frog sunglasses and frog stapler. I even threw in my World Wildlife tree frog T-shirt on principle, though I would soon be living in T-shirts and sweatshirts and it would have proved useful.

It was the first nice day in June and tons of people turned out. It was strange to watch what people would buy. Old Mrs. Murphy, for instance, who lived on the street behind ours. I'd have thought she'd have gone for pictures or china or cutlery, but she dived into a box of square carpet pieces as if it was gold. We didn't know what to charge for what we really thought of as garbage, so she reached into her purse and handed us five dollars with a big grin on her face.

"Just the thing," she said.

My mum suggested Matt carry the box of bits to her house for her, which he did, earning another dollar.

My excellent frog collection sold out, of course, but not as a set. It was strange to see it dwindle frog by frog. We sold sheets and towels and ends of paint. We sold golf clubs (my dad had to go inside while my mum negotiated the deal) and two woks and a lava lamp that I didn't even know my parents had and might have wanted had I known but it was too late.

We made eight hundred dollars that day and the house looked better. Not empty at all, because there was still big furniture and appliances. Just really, really tidy.

With the money we made on the yard sale, we bought really good backpacks. Very clever backpacks with smaller removable packs attached by zippers and Velcro to the main ones. Mine was green and black—a final tribute to the frogs I was leaving behind.

Unbeknownst to all of us, Matt had held back his skateboard. Not only had he not sold it, he wouldn't let it go into storage.

"What are you going to do with a skateboard in the Australian outback?" I asked.

"Carry it till I find some pavement," he said.

Dad really protested. If he'd given up his golf clubs he didn't see why Matt couldn't give up his skateboard. He could always buy one later. Matt argued that while golf clubs needed a golf course, a skateboard could be useful transportation.

"So long as you carry it, then," Mum said. "I'm not."

"Me neither."

"Me neither!"

When there were just fifteen sleeps left, the big things started to go. Some men arrived with a truck and walked in and looked around and offered a thousand dollars for the living-room and dining-room furniture. I knew my mum had paid a thousand dollars just for the couch. They took the couch and two matching chairs and the wood chairs with the woven backs and the coffee table and the hutch and the dining-room table and six matching chairs and the little end tables and the two standing lamps.

The walnut bureau was not part of that deal. It was special to my mum because it was her first "serious grown-up" purchase, bought before she even met my dad. It was definitely an antique. Everyone who knew about that sort of thing would admire it when they came in the house. "Burl walnut," they'd say. Then they'd usually rub their fingers lightly over the top and my mum would grin proudly. My dad was for putting it in storage, but Mum seemed to think that giving up this one thing would be proof of her good intentions. We were paring down. We were lightening up. The bureau had to go.

Poor mum. Every antique dealer offered her the same price. The last one to come by had those half glasses that sat down on his nose. He peered over his little specs and said, "Five hundred." This time my mum protested.

"It's worth five times that!"

"If you're willing to wait five years to find the right customer..."

She took the five hundred.

After the big stuff went, the house didn't look tidy, it just looked empty.

We got fifty for the computer, twenty-five for the lawnmower (which couldn't go in the garage sale because dad wanted to keep the grass cut until the last minute) and twenty-five for the vacuum cleaner.

Our last sleep in the house, we ate take-out chicken and coleslaw with plastic forks in the middle of the naked living room. Matt and I had half a day of school the next day—our last—during which the Goodwill people would arrive to clear out the mattresses we'd been having our last few sleeps on.

The morning at school was kind of emotional. There was a party for me during last class. Because everyone knew the whole purpose of the adventure was *not* to accumulate, there were no little frog gifts or anything that would have to be packed away or carried or in any way held on to. Instead of a card they all signed a balloon and instead of a gift everyone had pitched in some money to buy me a tiny little packable roll of one hundred stamps. I promised to send a postcard from every exotic location, not realizing at the time that the stamps wouldn't work from exotic locations outside Canada.

I heard "I'll miss you" and "write to me" a lot but mostly I heard "your parents are so cool" and "I wish my parents would do something like this." I wonder. Anyway, it was a real huggie fest, even with Laurie. I didn't get out of there without crying.

When we met back at the naked house we didn't have too much time to get misty over leaving it. A huge moving van had arrived and was backed into the driveway. It had taken us sixty days to clear out our stuff. It would take the new people about sixty minutes to fill it up again. Out came a couch, a couple of lazy-boy chairs, a TV, a dining-room set. And boxes and boxes with black lettering designating KITCHEN, LIVING-ROOM, MASTER BEDROOM, DOWNSTAIRS BATHROOM.

Now what?

My mum produced four money belts. She'd been going to get fanny packs when she'd read that they were "an invitation to thieves," and so she opted instead for these. In each one there was a laminated list of emergency phone numbers and information. Like I said, organized. Except for the phone numbers, these were individualized cards with each of our names, dates of birth and, where applicable, social insurance numbers across the top. It wasn't until I got that little card that I knew my blood type was A positive. Thanks, Mum.

We had already all got our passports. These were going to be kept in Mum's backpack, but I pushed for Matt and me getting to keep our own in our money belts and with us at all times. I won.

We stood there. Mum did her isn't-this-exciting hissing between her teeth, *tsssss*. Dad opened his eyes wide and nodded. Matt shifted from foot to foot. I waited.

"We should hitchhike out of town," Matt finally said.

"Hitchhike?" Mum's frown line appeared. "Is that safe?"

"Safe enough with the four of us," Dad said, "but who's going to pick up a family of four?"

"I thought we'd bus and train and plane," Mum said.

"Our money would last longer if we did a little hitching, Elly."

"I thought we weren't going to worry about money. 'When we run out we run out.'"

35

"Yes, but—"

"Hey, whoa!" I broke in. "Let's get off the lawn!"

We turned and took one last look at the house. Two movers were carrying a huge mattress through the front door.

"Goodbye, house!" someone said, and then we all did it. "Goodbye, house!"

A bus pulled up just then and Matt stepped half in and talked to the driver.

"Does this go to the city bus station?"

"Sure does," she said, and practically before he'd turned to see if we wanted to take the bus, we were piling in behind him, Mum going *tsssss*. I've never seen someone so excited about riding a bus.

We wound in and around every little street. Old ladies carrying bags got on wearing buttoned sweaters even though it was warm out. Finally, we pulled out onto the highway and ten minutes later we were in the city. Soon after that we pulled into the bus station.

"Goodbye, Bus Driver!" my mum said. If I'd known she could get so much pleasure out of riding the bus, I'd have given her a month's worth of tickets instead of all those chocolates and bath beads and perfume.

Well, now we were really up against it.

"I say we just go in and get the first bus out of here," I said.

"Or should we get the first bus that leaves on the half hour?"

"Or should we get the first bus that goes to a place beginning with S?"

"Shouldn't we have some vague idea about where we're going?"

"No, that's the point! We don't know where we're going."

"Is that the point? I thought the point was to try things we've never tried before."

"Well, I've never tried just walking into a bus station and getting on a bus and I want to try that."

"Okay."

"Okay."

"Okay."

Whew. For four people who knew two weeks in advance what they would be eating for dinner on a given night, this was exhausting. We ended up taking a couple of rooms in a Holiday Inn, pigging out at an all-you-can-eat buffet, having hot baths and flopping into bed. We decided that when we gathered together at breakfast the next day, we would really, truly this time, do something crazy. Really.

SEVEN

"What are you having for breakfast, Mum?"

She looked at me over the top of the gigantic plasticized menu with bold arrows pointing here and there and colourful pictures of food. Every morning of their lives my parents had two bran muffins. No raisins to stick to the dental work. Plain bran. Every morning.

"Waffles," she said, folding the menu shut.

Matt and I had waffles, too, and Dad impressed us all by ordering the Hungry Man's Breakfast and all the cholesterol that entailed. His toast was thickly sliced and the home fries were piled so high they were begging for help. So Matt and I helped—Matt going for the biggest ones, me going for the crispiest.

It was Mum, naturally, who came up with our loose—not at all rigid, nothing we had to stick by or anything, nothing that couldn't be changed or modified—plan of action. She started tearing little strips off the cleanest part of her paper placemat. She gave one to each of us, then handed Matt a ballpoint pen.

"Write down something you'd really love to do, Matt."

Matt hesitated. "Are we all going to?"

"Yes," Mum said.

"Then we all have to do it at once," he said. "Otherwise I'll think too much."

Mum produced another pen and a couple of pencils from her pack. We were all poised over our strips of placemat.

"Okay, okay. Money's no object?"

"Money's no object...obviously, we can't go to the moon."

"Who wants to go to the moon?"

"Not me."

"Not me."

"I *would* go, but I don't especially want to go, if you know what I mean. If a genie said three wishes, I wouldn't waste one on the moon."

"Same here."

"Exactly."

"So, three...two..."

"Wait! Do we all have to do what the other three want to do?"

"We all have to go there, but we don't all have to do the thing."

"Okay, that's fair."

"That's fair."

"Okay, three...two..."

"Wait! Just kidding. Okay."

"Three...two...one."

We all hunched over our strips. Just writing it

down was exciting enough for my mother. She was hissing like crazy while she folded up her strip.

"You're all going to be surprised," she said. "I don't care. It's not like me, but...I don't care. *Tsssss*."

Then came the problem of reading the strips. Should we just read them out loud right now? Should we hand them to the person on our right to read? Who would go first?

"Dad should go first," Matt said. "It's his mid-life crisis."

"I think we should read one," Dad said, "and not know what the others are. Keep it a surprise."

"Ooh."

"Why not?"

"Throw them all in a hat," I said, "and pick one."

"Ooh."

"Here's the hat," Matt said, whipping off his cap. We all placed our tightly folded strips in the hat.

"Who picks?"

"Dad should."

"Why me?"

Fortunately, the waitress came up and we got her in on it. She reached into the hat as calmly as you please and pulled out one of the little wads. No one reached over to take it from her, so she placed it on the table near the salt and pepper.

"Will that be all?" she asked.

Mum and Dad nodded. The waitress wrote the

total on our bill and turned it upside down in front of Dad, then went away. I knew the strip wasn't mine, but I didn't know whose it was. I went to reach for it.

"Wait a minute," Matt said. "What if this gets read out, you know, and it's, like, in Mexico or something, and I know that mine is closer—not that it is, but I'm just saying—shouldn't we do mine first?"

"No way," I said. "Then we might as well all just read out our wishes and do them in order."

Matt looked at the parents.

"Really?"

"Really. That's what this is all about."

So I unfolded the wad and read it. And it wasn't Matt's. It was Dad's, after all.

I WANT TO BUNGEE JUMP OFF THAT BRIDGE IN B.C.

EIGHT

I was certainly glad we had established that we all
have to *go* there, but we don't all have to *do* the thing
rule, because there was no way I wanted to bungee
jump at all, let alone off a bridge and into a river.

The remaining three strips of placemat were put in
a shiny red plastic pill case bought for an outrageous-
ly inflated price because we bought it in a gift shop in
the Holiday Inn and not in a proper drug store. We
sealed it with two bandaids and entrusted it to Mum's
pack. In a way I envied Dad because he had three sur-
prises left and the rest of us now had only two.

We flew to Vancouver. I like the way that sounds,
"we flew to Vancouver." It was Matt's and my first
plane ride ever. The seats were arranged so that there
were rows of two near the windows and three down
the middle. Matt and I got a window and Mum and
Dad got seats in the section of three just across the
aisle from us. The man in the third seat pulled down
his little tray that's stuck onto the seat in front and
whipped out a laptop. How could anyone work
when there was so much to look at?

A lot of the stewardesses were actually men—
flight attendants—and they came by offering tiny

pillows and blankets and headsets. We took everything that was offered to us. I even took a magazine which I never read. I knew my mum wasn't crazy about flying, and every now and then I heard my dad say, "Breathe, Elly," and there would be a long exhalation of held-in air from the middle seat.

The flight attendant went through a safety routine, but it was all so fast I didn't really take it in. His face was absolutely expressionless while some voice from somewhere talked in English and French about lights that came on in an emergency and seat belts and oxygen falling from the ceiling, and he pointed at all these emergency things with the index fingers of each hand. Seatbelts tightened, tabletops up, seat backs up and you're ready.

Take-off was so great. One moment you're barrelling along a runway and then, whump, you're suspended over all the houses and wires and cars and the plane is tipped way, way up. My mum didn't really get back to breathing regularly till we were levelled out again. That was at thirty-five thousand feet, but it didn't take us too long to get there I must say. Captain Taylor's voice came over the speaker and welcomed us aboard, in English and French, and said he was anticipating a smooth flight.

"I'll bet they say that every time," I heard my mum whisper to my dad, but she looked okay, really. And the man beside her had already lowered his table and was, again, working away on his laptop.

I'd already seen the in-flight movie, which wasn't on a movie screen but a tiny monitor that poked down out of the ceiling. I watched it again anyway and noticed that they'd substituted "freakin'" for a certain word and "shoot" for another word and even cut out an entire scene.

The food was great. The attendants slid trays out of a metal trolley and on the trays were a roll and butter and a little plastic compartment with chicken and rice and snowpea pods and another little compartment with cake, a salad in clear plastic and a cup with its own little depression in the tray so it wouldn't slosh around. The cutlery—real metal not plastic—came in its own skinny envelope. Before we knew it Captain Taylor was telling us to put our watches back and look out either side to see the Rockies. Wow. They looked a little unreal, like the relief map the whole class made in grade eight geography. It looked like the snow had been put on with a caulking gun, like we'd done it, and the lakes seemed like our tiny mirrors only murkier. The trees weren't as easily discernible as they had been in ours. And then they just all of a sudden ended. No more Rockies.

It wasn't too long before Captain Taylor was talking to us again.

"It's a perfect day in Vancouver," he said.

They took away our little pillows, our thin blankets and our headsets. The fasten-your-seatbelt sign came on. Tabletops up, seat backs up. We landed, my mum exhaled and we were flushed along to the baggage carousel with all our fellow travellers. People who hadn't said a word to each other on the plane were now wishing each other a pleasant visit or a welcome home. It was as if they stayed in their own little worlds on the plane because they were afraid they'd get stuck in a four-hour conversation with someone boring or something, but now that it was safe and there was no chance of being put upon, everyone was very nice. Even Laptop, who hadn't said two words to my mum the whole flight, started asking all kinds of questions. Were we from Vancouver or just visiting? And for how long? Enjoy your stay.

"That place in B.C." turned out to be on Vancouver Island. No problem, ferries left for the island practically every hour. We could catch a bus right at the airport that would cross over on the ferry. Piece of cake. Except that you didn't exactly catch a bus at the airport, you caught the shuttle bus, which pulled in at two different hotels and let you off at the second hotel where you bought your ticket for the bus. No problem. Except that the first shuttle was packed full so we stood around for ten minutes and got the next one. We got out at the Delta Pacific and found that the next big bus would be about forty-five minutes. The girl behind the desk was very perky with a very big smile.

"Do you want to buy your return tickets now?"

Unbeknownst to her, this threw us into a major tizzy. *Did* we want to buy return tickets? We didn't know. It would mean saving three dollars each, but...where was our next destination? We weren't sure. How could we decide whether to return to Vancouver, the city, without giving away any of our choices? We stood aside and let about ten people buy their tickets while we dithered. We opted for one way. Who knew? Maybe once we were over there someone's choice would send us to Japan or Alaska or something.

So we sat around for three-quarters of an hour in the lobby of the Delta Pacific, then caught the bus that drove to the ferry. There was a huge lineup waiting for that ferry, cars backed up forever with people standing around outside or stretched out on the hoods, dogs on leashes being walked up and down the pavement. We breezed on by them in our bus right onto the lower deck which reeked of bus-gas fumes. We memorized the number of our bus and climbed up to Deck 5.

The ferry was called *Spirit of British Columbia,* and it had everything from cubicles and photocopying machines for the workaholics to jungle gym areas for the toddlers. I spent most of my time outside where, every now and then, the blast of the horn made me jump out of my skin. Especially as we approached the Gulf Islands. When we rounded a bend the horn blasted and then an answering horn and there was another ferry, just like us, heading the other way.

I was practically the only non-smoking person outside. Why would anybody miss this? It was so beautiful. I couldn't get enough of the hilly islands rounding down to a little lighthouse and then, the water. After a quick tour around the deck Matt had gone in to play the machines in the arcade, and Mum was sitting at a table writing postcards home. Even Dad was inside "psyching himself up" for the big jump.

However, by the time the bus rolled into Victoria, even I was starting to sag. It had taken us as long to get from the airport to here as it had taken us to fly from home to Vancouver. We needed to collapse. But where? After that first Holiday Inn experience we'd held a conference and decided that hotels and motels should be avoided unless absolutely necessary. Mum did an inexplicable *tsssss* over this issue, which seemed like a nervous hiss at the time but which later took on more meaning.

So we stayed in the hostel in Victoria—Mum and me in one room and Dad and Matt in another. I was practically asleep before I'd even unzipped my bag.

NINE

There's nothing like a twelve-hour sleep to restore energy. Whereas at the end of the day before we'd felt like dishrags, now we were adventurers again. We went to a place called Rent-A-Wreck and rented a car that was a lot less of a wreck than either of our old ones. The drive was easy—there's just this one highway that heads up island—and beautiful. Every now and then we'd get a glimpse of water and snow-capped mountains through the trees as they whizzed by.

It didn't feel long at all but it was probably about an hour later that we saw a big sign saying BUNGY ZONE, HAVE A LOOK. I'd always thought it was spelled with a double e. We turned off onto a road that dipped down and around and up under the sign itself. There was one of those warnings in much smaller print that said something to the effect that if you had diabetes, heart disease or were pregnant you'd better not do this and anyway whatever happened it wasn't their fault.

My mum exhaled and we drove into the woods. There was another sign saying BUSH WALK TO BUNGY ZONE, but we opted for staying in the car and after a few turns there it was before us. Bungy Zone. Dad parked in front of a cabin-like structure with a red steel roof. Mum and Matt and I couldn't take our eyes off the big steel bridge that went up, up, up via three sets of steel stairs. Even from where we were sitting the bridge seemed high, but that was just the half of it. We were at the edge of a wide chasm, a gorge, and so the actual plunge was even longer than what we could see. It made my stomach flip just to think of it, actually.

While my dad went in to find out about procedure, Matt and I approached the stairs. They were those see-through stairs. Not the part you step on but the part that usually rises up to the next stair. Nothing. I think if I hadn't been able to see through the stairs I'd have at least been able to climb up there. Mum, of course, could barely look up so I wasn't put to the test. I would stay with Mum, and Matt would climb with Dad.

Dad came out of the cabin. He'd already paid for his jump. He'd already committed.

"I could get an all-day pass for three hundred dollars," he said. This time it was me who told my mum to breathe.

Her plan was to stay in the cabin. We went in, but there was a TV showing, of course, an endless tape of bungy jumpers. I thought she was going to be sick.

Outside again I suggested she wait in the car, but

she kind of thrust her shoulders back and said, no, she would watch. We saw that Dad and Matt were on the third tier of steps and we walked straight ahead to the edge of the cliff where there was a chain-link fence. Mum wouldn't look down. She just plastered a fake grin on her face and kept looking up at Dad. I looked down. Whoa. There was a red rubber dinghy down in the water and the water itself was very dark and still. Tall fir trees jutted up all around us on each side of the chasm and directly behind Mum and me there were two trees with very red-looking bark. The white rope—the bungy cord itself—was hanging in several loops from the centre of the bridge, and it looked fuzzy and frayed to me. Needless to say I didn't say this out loud. Out loud I kept saying things like, "He'll be fine, this is great, heck, tons of people do this every day." In fact there weren't that many people. The pamphlet we'd picked up in the cabin showed people lined up all along the bridge and partway down the stairs, but today there wasn't exactly a crowd.

When the first person jumped I was surprised how calmly my mum took it and that's when I saw that her eyes were closed. Her head was lifted, she was smiling broadly and waving occasionally, but her eyes were squeezed shut.

Dad was the very last in the small group, right behind a woman wearing a shiny purple blouse, black pants and high heels, of all things. I couldn't help wondering what would happen if one of her heels got caught and she was left hanging there, probably with a broken leg, from the bridge.

Once you jumped, and had finished bobbing, you caught a long pole held by the person in the boat and were swung over to the edge where you were untied. Then you had to climb up flights of totally see-through stairs to get to Mum's and my level again.

It turned out my fears about the woman in the heels were a little hasty. She went to the edge and the two guys counted to three. One...two...three. No jump. She changed her mind and decided that instead of being dipped into the river slightly—which was an option available to the individual jumper—she wanted to pull up short above the water. They readjusted the cord while my poor dad waited. She went to the edge again. One...two...three. No jump. She decided that instead of going forward—too awful—she would go backwards. Better to see where she'd been than where she was going, I guess. She backed up close to the edge. Her shiny purple blouse was glinting beneath the harness which had hiked her slacks up to reveal the ankles above the high heels. The two guys counted again. One...two...three... for the third and last time. You only got three chances to back away, or else people would stand there chickening out all day. She balked. "Three" had come and gone for the third time and she hadn't jumped. In fact, she not only hadn't jumped, on the count of three she kneeled down and crawled away from the edge of the bridge on her hands and knees. I didn't blame her one bit.

It was my dad's turn. I watched as he stepped onto something which he later told us was a weigh scale. I watched as one of the guys wrapped some thick white towels around his calves and attached the strap and the clasp which were attached to the bungy cord. I watched as he moved to the very edge of the bridge. Even though I couldn't see the details of Matt's face, I could tell by the way he stood that he was feeling great up there. It was like he was Dad's second or something.

I imagined Dad backing away a couple of times, maybe even backing out altogether. I'd never known him to do anything but golf. He was never much of a swimmer and I'd never seen him dive.

He spread his arms, he bent slightly at the knees...and that's the last I saw. I closed my eyes, too. I heard him, though. There was this long drawn-out *Eeeeyyeeaahhh!* that seemed to go on forever and then a series of *ho-ho-hos* which I figured were accompanying the sproings and twirls as he dangled at the end of the cord.

Once we knew he'd done it, my mum and I opened our eyes. Dad was hanging upside down reaching for the pole and missing it, laughing and reaching for it again. Matt was coming down the three flights of stairs saying, "Yes, yes, yes!"

When we all met Dad at the top of the see-through stairs, his hair and upper body were soaked.

"You dipped!"

"He dipped!"

"I dipped!"

"Oh, Gary!"

"Way to go, Dad!"

"Lookin' good, Dad!"

He'd done it. He'd not only done it, he'd done it on the first count, bound at the ankles instead of in a harness, face first with his arms out to the sides like birdie wings.

The legs were a little shaky, the knees a little weak, but he looked happy.

And he couldn't stop talking about it! He told us over and over again what we'd already seen—how the woman in purple kept changing her mind and then finally crawled away. How he'd gone on the first jump. How he'd spread his arms and just flown out over the river. How he'd bobbed back up just after his head touched water. How great Wayne and Steve were at judging just how much cord he should have. He turned back and looked up at Wayne and Steve and gave them a thumbs-up sign. He kept saying "BUN-GY!" at odd intervals throughout the rest of the day.

TEN

"We should celebrate," Dad said.

"We should go to the Empress Hotel for tea," Mum said.

We all looked at her. Clearly the bungy experience called for more of a beer and wings kind of celebration. But Mum was looking a lot shakier than Dad—wan, to tell the truth—and we all instinctively felt that a quiet afternoon tea was something we could tolerate for the sake of her nerves. Even Matt.

"Why not?" he said with a shrug.

As we curved down and around and up and out onto the highway we all said it simultaneously,

"Bye, Bungy Zone!"

The drive back to Victoria seemed faster than the drive up. We knew how to get to the hotel because it was right beside the bus station we'd landed at the night before. It's a huge old building, the kind you'd call imposing.

"Bun-gy!" Dad said as we went inside.

The tea room wasn't really a tea room. It was in the lobby of the hotel. The lobby was big and had old-fashioned furniture and patterned rugs and pillars from floor to ceiling. Dad was just saying he could taste the crumpets when we were stopped dead in our tracks by a woman with her hair parted in the middle wearing a red suit and gold and pearl earrings.

"Tea for four, please," my mum said.

"I'm sorry," the red suit said. "We have a dress code." Except she didn't look sorry, she looked determined. As if we weren't going to get past her lectern dressed like *that*. There was a long silence while we all just looked at her. She was already looking over our shoulders at the couple who was coming in behind us. The man was wearing a suit and the woman was wearing a dress.

"A dress code for *tea*?" my mum said, at which point my dad took her by the elbow muttering about how that was okay we'd go somewhere else.

Matt and I looked around. Everyone was dressed like the man and woman behind us: suits and dresses. And tea was being brought to them in silver teapots. And the crumpets came on three-tiered little silver trays.

We'd never been turned away from anywhere before and it felt a little weird. I mean, it's not like we weren't clean or anything. I thought my mum might be gearing up for a scene, but nothing could dampen Dad's mood.

"Bun-gy!"

Not five minutes later we were in a donut shop. No dress code. Matt and I chose hot chocolate and donuts with sprinkles. Our companions enjoyed double double coffees and honey crullers. But the best part was, soon after we were settled, a couple of guys came through the door who'd also done the bungy jump that morning. They recognized Dad immediately and after they got their coffee they brought it over to the table next to ours.

"Elly, Steph, Matt, this is Don and Jim."

As soon as we were all introduced, Don and Jim and Dad looked at each other and did it simultaneously.

"Bun-gy!"

Don and Jim were not the kind of men my dad usually hung around with. They were guys. Kind of beefy looking. Tough. Every now and then Don or Jim would reach over and pound a fist into my dad's shoulder. He was loving it.

They went over it all again. How purple got the count—one, two, three—then "crawled outta there, eh?" How Dad and Don and Jim had gone by their ankles because that was the "pure experience." How Wayne and Steve were so good at their job and knew just how much cord to give you so you could dip or stay dry.

"Dip or stay dry?"

"Bun-gy!"

They exchanged names and phone numbers—Dad gave the number of some close friends back home and said they'd know where to reach him. When they finally parted, Dad had a huge grin on his face.

"Great pair of guys," he said. To which there was only one response.

"Bun-gy!"

Mum took the red pill case out of her pack and put it on the table. I reached over and took off the bandaids, sticking them to the side of the table, hanging down, so we wouldn't lose them. Matt twisted the top off and held it to Dad.

"Okay, Dad, you can choose now because you've had your turn already."

Dad reached his hand out, then pulled it back.

"I can't," he said. "Let's always have someone else do it."

"Excuse me," he said to a man who was sweeping the floor—I must say we were all getting a little less self-conscious with each passing day—"would you mind choosing one of these?"

The man looked a little puzzled, especially when the pill box didn't contain pills, but he stuck two big fingers into the pill box. Then he started to unfold the paper.

"No," my dad said. "It's not for you, it's for us."

"For you?"

"Yes, thank you. We just didn't want to have to choose."

The guy looked at Dad and shrugged. "Okay," he said, handing over the little scrunched piece of paper.

"Thank you," Dad said, turning back to us with his eyes wide. "Next time, let's put them in the cap again."

"Sure, but there'll only be two in the cap."

"All the same...the pill box is a little daunting, I think."

"A whole hat isn't?"

"But you can't really see into the whole hat."

"Can you read that out, please?"

"I'll bet it's Steph's."

But I already could tell that it wasn't mine. Dad spread the slip out on the table so we could all crane our necks and read it at the same time. Even before I finished reading, I heard my mum's *tsssss*.

I WANT TO GO TO LAS VEGAS IN A RED SEQUINED DRESS

ELEVEN

I'm not going to go into our lengthy deliberations over whether this red dress should be bought in Las Vegas (Matt's and my vote) or Victoria (Mum's and Dad's). They won and we bought in Victoria, and it probably turned out just as well because we *all* had to be outfitted for Vegas, except Matt, and the stores there were ridiculously expensive. I was going to go for a slinky gold number when I caught myself. This was Mum's fantasy, so I chose a slinky but very simple pant and tunic combo in crushed velvet. Dad bought a navy blazer to wear with his own jeans and shirt and—no kidding—a western-style tie ending in two dangly silver-tipped points.

It turned out our dithering over whether or not to buy return ferry tickets wasn't wasted because there was an airport right on Vancouver Island—Victoria Airport, except that it wasn't in Victoria at all but in a little town called Sidney just fifteen minutes away. We could drive there and leave our rental car at the airport. That way we wouldn't have to lug all our shopping bags and Matt's skateboard onto a bus.

Because we got the first flight available, we flew to Seattle. Just a short hop, really. My poor mum had practically only exhaled from the takeoff when she had to hold her breath again for the landing. We clambered off the plane with our boxes, picked up our backpacks at the carousel and then got our passports stamped going through customs. Our first stamp! In Seattle we got a flight straight to Las Vegas, Nevada.

It was weird not having the safety directions done in French. And this time instead of watching a flight attendant, we watched a video showing big fat arrows pointing to all the exits, floor lights and oxygen masks. Once in the air, though, everything was the same—seats back, belts off and tables down. I've discovered I'm a good traveller. I like not knowing what I'm going to get to eat. And I like trading compartments of plane food. I'll give up one of those jellied desserts for an extra bun with butter any day.

Matt was grumpy the whole flight though. He made me squeeze out into the aisle at least three times so he could go to the bathroom and I know he didn't really have to go, he was just restless.

I finally hit on a game we hadn't played in years, not since I used to babysit him. We called it line-at-a-time story. Someone begins with one line—and the first line always begins "once upon a time"—and the other does the next line and so on. I started.

"Once upon a time and far, far, away..."

"A death-star exploded near the planet Zamar..."

"But one loving, gentle Zamarian mother named Elda..."

"Wearing a green gilk-hide dress, all gungy and torn..."

"Bundled her baby boy—"

"Masher!"

"Bundled her baby boy, Masher, in the softest gilk-hide she could find..."

Somehow, despite the fact that there was a war on Zamar in addition to the death-star exploding nearby, Masher got sent out in a hideously ugly space-pod which landed on a beautiful green and blue planet. He had some unsettling experiences, but eventually he met up with people who liked him, even liked his extra toes and fingers. They took him in.

"And he lived, of course..."

"Happily ever after."

Babysitters everywhere, go right ahead. All I ask is ten percent of your gross.

The story took a long time, but its effect didn't last.

"What's there gonna be for me to do there?"

I was on the verge of telling him to stop whining and had closed my eyes pretending to sleep, when I heard him say quietly beside me, "Cool."

I leaned over. We were landing in Vegas at night and, as everyone knows—though I didn't, really—

Las Vegas, Nevada, is right in the middle of the desert. So when you land at night there's this handful of glitz thrown down in the blackness—like a molten splash against the dark.

TWELVE

The reason for Mum's *tsssss* over the discussion about hotels vs. hostels was immediately apparent. Only the night before we'd heated up two large cans of beans in a battered and scorched pot in the Victoria Hostel and now here we were in a "suite." All part of the experience.

Matt and I had our own rooms that opened onto a living area with a sunken TV nook and huge sliding glass doors through which neon lights were winking and blinking and flashing constantly. Mum and Dad's bedroom opened onto this area, too, but from the opposite side, and their room was much fancier than ours. They had their own personal jacuzzi bathtub and double sink in their bathroom. Matt and I had an adjoining bathroom with only one sink, but it was still fancier than any bathroom I'd ever seen in real life.

"What's that?" he asked.

It was a bidet. Now, I knew what it was for—one of my friends' parents even had one—but I just didn't feel like explaining it to Matt at that moment. I shrugged. He went into the parents' bathroom. They had one, too.

"What's that?" he asked.

"That's to wash your socks in," my dad said.

"Gary," my mother said.

"You'll notice, son," Dad said, "that this particular item is situated between the toilet and the bath? Well, that's what it is...something between a toilet and a bath."

"A urinal?"

"For heaven's sake, Gary," my mother said. "You sit on it like a toilet, Matt, but you don't go in it, you use it to clean...you know."

"Oh," Matt said. Then, "Ohhh."

The rest of our suite was not so alien, just very plush. Everything in Las Vegas that wasn't actually lit had a kind of shimmery quality to it, like the bungy woman's purple blouse.

Or Mum's red dress. She took it out of its box before she unpacked anything else and hung it up. She hung it from the curtain rod so the lights from the neon signs sparkled off every individual sequin. We ordered in pizza and sat in the sunken part of the suite with the red dress hanging over us. Mum was wondering what different shows she might go to. Paul Anka was a big draw, of course, but so was Wayne Newton.

"We can do them all!" my dad said.

Matt was getting gloomier and gloomier. We went to bed stuffed and tired after each one of us had had a hot bath. Once again, we all slept longer than we would have ever thought possible.

The next afternoon Mum and I went down to the beauty salon in the hotel. Matt was told he could explore the hotel but couldn't leave it. Mum made him repeat our room number and code knock over and over again. The code knock was the beginning of the Do Re Mi song rapped out with the proper beat up to the words "a female deer." You had to pause and count slowly to five before you repeated this.

WELCOME TO THE ESTHETIC EXPERIENCE was the sign that blinked digitally at us as we entered the salon. The Esthetic Experience provided whole body grooming from head to toe. Hair to pedicure. I naturally was pushing for the works but my mum has always been a lip gloss and mascara person so it was enough to get her to agree to poofy hair and makeup. She plunged bravely into the heavily perfumed, gold-accented white room. Actually, the boutique itself was no more flashy than most makeup counters at Eaton's, but the clientele...well.

There was a woman in there who had to be seven feet tall, and that's before she put on her peacock headdress. I'm not kidding. Above her corn-rowed bangs there was a bejewelled peacock head, three-dimensional and jutting forward in line with her nose. Spreading out from the head was a shiny metallic stylized set of wings studded with clear rhinestones, and fanning out above all this were the feathers of the peacock's tail. Ruby, sapphire, emerald and topaz rhinestones formed the eyes with some black stone, probably onyx, at the centre of each eye. Her dress was gold and her arms bare except for two jewel-encrusted cuffs on her wrists. A showgirl, obviously. All she bought was a lipstick, which cost more than my weekly allowance, then she glided away from us.

The woman who "did" my mother was named Tanya. The first thing she tackled was the lips—nice and smooth after all those years of gloss. She rolled out a Lipstick Library with too many choices and too many names. She saw my mother heading for a slump and said, "Should I just do you?"

"Yes, please," my mum said, and while no doubt this speeded things up tremendously, we were still in there for thirty-five minutes. There was an all-over bronzing product to prepare her palette. There was concealer and liner for her eyes. The lips got dusted with powder, then three different products were applied to them: basecoat, lipstick, lip liner, more lipstick. And Tanya took her time, dabbing here, smoothing there, smudging and blending.

At one point, just as I was getting mesmerized by this process of making up Mum, one of the other women in the store yelled, "Bride!" Heads turned, and sure enough outside the boutique a woman in white went whizzing by, her veil floating in front of us for a moment, then vanishing.

"A showgirl, right?" I said to Tanya.

"No. A bride. They get married, then go shopping," Tanya said.

What was interesting was that when Tanya had finished, my mum actually looked good. Not all phoney and made-up like a showgirl but sparkly and good. Considering the layers and number of products on her face, the look was kind of subtle. Of course out in the light of day it would probably have looked awful, but inside with all those lights and mirrors it seemed right.

We didn't actually buy any of the makeup, which was a disappointment to Tanya. While we sat there, women were ringing up purchases of over two hundred dollars on a regular basis. When Mum wouldn't buy makeup, Tanya tried to sell her sunblock, herbal eye-pads and eye-drops, saying how her skin would be stripped by the Strip: minimum temperatures of 105 degrees Fahrenheit outside, smoke and fluorescent light and air-conditioning inside.

"You can't just rely on the misters," she said.

The misters are lined up outside the shopping areas, and they're supposed to cool the shoppers without actually getting anyone soaking. As if that's not weird enough, it turns out they also pipe oxygen into the casinos to keep your energy level up.

Dad had finished showering and was shaving when we went back up to the room. I think during the whole Vegas experience, Mum got the most value for her money out of The Dress. The dress was very simple—long sleeved, off the shoulder, falling straight from just below the armpits to the floor—but it was, after all, red sequins. Every time she moved, she threw off sparkles.

The most spectacular moment was her Entrance. Real movie-star stuff. First she appeared at the door to their room. Then she sashayed towards us—three half turns and a wiggle—before sprawling on the couch, legs crossed, tossing her hair and smoking a fake cigarette. Then she collapsed into hisses and giggles.

When she left, on Dad's arm, she turned and blew a kiss.

THIRTEEN

I could just imagine Mum slinking into a casino on Dad's arm. Heads would turn. *Who is that woman with the poofy hair and the devastating dress?* She wouldn't even bother with the slot machines, not her. The slot machines were for people in velvet pants and shiny jackets that said I LOVE NEW YORK. Mum would start with blackjack. She would coolly look up at the dealer, sweating already in his white shirt and black tie because he would know anyone in a dress like that was A Player.

"I'll hold," she'd say, having barely lifted the card to see it.

The dealer sticks on nineteen. The man to her right and the man to her left shove their cards away in disgust. Mum flips hers over. A queen and an ace. Blackjack.

Before long whispers begin to circulate around the casino about the Queen of Hearts, the woman in the red dress who never loses. She slinks away from the blackjack table and tries her hand at roulette. It's the same story. Chips keep coming her way and she piles them up, betting the whole bundle each time on red. And winning each time.

Soon people are trying to get near her in the hope that a little of her luck will rub off on them. Now and then she deigns to shake a hand or blow on a pair of dice. Red dice, of course. Men in tuxedos send complimentary bottles of champagne. A thousand pairs of eyes are attuned to her every move.

One pair of those eyes belongs to Benny, a swarthy character known for his luck. Benny the Bidder, they call him. Only Benny, unlike the Queen of Hearts, relies on a little more than luck. Benny knows all the angles—which dealers are weak and which are strong—and he never does anything stupid like palming cards or sneaking in loaded dice. He doesn't need to. Benny has friends. He knows everybody, and this dame, this Queen of Hearts, is muscling in on his territory.

"Check her out," he says, almost inaudibly, to the bland-looking man beside him.

Bland checks her out. He follows her from table to table. Blackjack, baccarat, five-card stud. She touches her earring. A signal? No. She never does it again. The skinny guy in the hick tie, is he in on it somehow? He touches her elbow, he pecks her on the cheek, he wears a permanent grin...but none of these things are signals.

At the roulette table she is a marvel. Chips pile up in front of her like little smokestacks.

"She's legit," Bland mutters to Benny.

Benny makes a decision. If you can't beat 'em, join 'em. He adjusts his tie. He stands a little straighter. He tells Bland to have a bottle of Dom Perignon sent over in three minutes. Just as he's about to make his move, Benny freezes. He's not the only one who's been watching this dame. A couple of blue suits—floor managers—have moved in on her. Skinny is making a fuss, but the suits brush him off like a fly.

The Queen of Hearts is taken to a room—ostensibly a room where she can count her chips in private—but there are even more suits in this room, and a bare lightbulb swinging from the ceiling.

"Well, well, well," a voice says.

"Three more holes in the ground," says the woman in red.

Silence.

Silence audible.

Then a knock at the door.

A signal.

The secret knock, rapped out to the tune of the Do Re Mi song.

I get up and open the door just a crack. Outside are Mum and Dad.

"What are you guys doing back so soon?"

Mum and Dad were back in our room. The Queen of Hearts *had* won at the roulette table, but there'd been no Benny, no Mr. Bland, no suits, no whisking her off into a secret room. When she made her first win she handed her original chips over to Dad with instructions not to give them back to her even if she begged. Then she made a little more money with her winnings and, likewise, handed him what she considered her starter chips. When she had been at it for awhile, each time making a modest little pile from her starter pile, she quit. That was it. She'd sat at a roulette table in a red sequined dress, looking very glitzy, and that was all she'd ever wanted to do.

My dad and I said to her almost at the same time, "How could you quit when you were on a roll?"

"That's precisely the time to quit," she said.

FOURTEEN

Darkness. Murmuring and the tinkling of glasses. We're sitting in banquettes of white in front of a semi-circular table. Us and hundreds of others like us, tiered so that we can all have a good view of— The Show.

Gradually, as the notes of a single oboe are heard throughout the room, the lights begin to rise not to their full extent but slightly, so that we're in a kind of twilight. Then...it's snowing.

Could this be? No. Yes. Mum and Dad and I look at each other. It must be confetti, right? Or teeny tiny plastic shavings. But as the stuff begins to land on our skin and instantly melt, we realize it really is snowing inside this showroom. Resisting the urge to stick out my tongue and catch some, I look around instead. It's a little like being right inside one of those glass things you hold in your hand and turn upside down to make it snow.

The oboe dies down and the lights dim again. My dad leans in and whispers, "It was just a technical problem they're having with the misters." Before my mum even has a chance to shush him, there's a musical "crash."

Down on the stage the curtains are pulling back to reveal an "ice rink" that looks like smooth tin foil. People are skating. Rollerblades, obviously, but from where we're sitting it's not hard to pretend they're real ice skates. These skaters are good, especially when you consider they don't exactly have a rink-size space to manoeuvre in. They twirl, they leap, they boogie to the very loud strains now of a full orchestra. It's like the Ice Capades right here in Las Vegas! There's even an Ice Queen in a white dress. She stands in a spotlight and sings and every now and then the spotlight changes colour and the white of her dress takes on the colour of the latest spot. She belts out a song about the coldness of her lover who has winter in his heart or something. My mum and dad are trying to figure out if this is a star.

"Who is that?"

"It's someone, isn't it?"

"Yes, but who?"

"It's...it's...ooh."

"Right! It's her. That's the one."

It turns out that after about an hour, when Winter has come and gone and we're finally in Fall, the only person we've recognized is the Peacock Lady from the Esthetic Experience, and I'm not sure that really counts.

The house lights go up after a bodiless voice has told us to hang in there for Bobby Blaze. That was just the opening act! All that hoopla and lighting and...snow, and it was just to whet our appetites for the real thing.

I'd never in my life heard the name Bobby Blaze, but my parents are going nuts.

"Ooh, Bobby," my mum says.

My dad squeezes my mum's shoulder and grins. Then he starts singing. Something along the lines of "I am yours, you are mine, won't you be my Valentine?"

Just when I'm beginning to think I shouldn't have come along on this date, my mum looks over and says, "We thought he was dead." This cracks us all up, but they're back in a reverent mood again by the time the house lights go down.

Darkness. No murmuring. No tinkling of glass. Silence. High above the stage a single spot of red. The spotlight widens until we can see an enormous heart. The heart starts to slowly descend until the pointy end of it is resting on a staircase delineated by tiny lights. The heart cracks, then falls open, and inside is a man in tight red pants and a white poet-style shirt, holding a hand mike. The crowd bursts into applause—some, like my parents, going so far as to pound on the tables in front of them.

When the adoration dies down, Bobby starts to sing.

I-uh

My mum's hands go up to her face.

AM-uh

My dad leans his head onto my mum's.

EUY-ors!

The music crashes wildly on *yours*, and Bobby's free hand is out now and he's starting down the steps, which stop their incessant twinkling and instead light up one at a time as his foot hits them.

You are mi-i-ine

Won't you be, oh, please be, baby, be

Be-uh

Be-uh

Be my Va-ha-len-tine!

Whoever this Bobby Blaze is, these are his people. The crowd loves him. He does some Elvis songs, even the Beatles, but what really gets the crowd going are those Bobby Blaze tunes.

Afterwards, my mum bombarded me with Blaze trivia.

"He's Canadian, you know."

"Really?"

"Well, no, not really. He was born in Florida but he went to high school in Winnipeg."

"He's a twin," my dad said.

"No, Gary, that was just a rumour."

My mum was having a wonderful time. She was looking all dreamy and goofy. Dad was taking some money out of his wallet. He handed it all to me.

"You and Matt might want to see a movie," he said.

Right. My job was to get Matt out of our room.

When I got back up there, he was slumped in front of the TV, both feet planted on his skateboard and mechanically moving it back and forth over the carpet. In the time it took me to cross over to the couch he must have clicked the remote three times.

I knew from years of handling Matt that my only hope was to remain relentlessly upbeat. If I once relaxed my guard and seemed exasperated with him, he had me.

"Okay!" I said, turning the TV off manually. "Let's do something!"

He gave me the most withering look, his legs on wheels moving back and forth between us. What worked at eleven was clearly not going to work at twelve.

"Okay, Matt, I'll come clean." I showed him the money. "Dad wants us to vamoose so he and Mum can have...."

"Have what?"

"...a romantic evening. Come on."

He groaned. He moaned. But he did get up off the couch.

"Matt," I said, "do you have to bring that?"

He had his skateboard under his arm.

"Yeah," he said. "I do."

Waiting for the elevator, he leaned up against the wall and spun the wheels with his left hand. He looked miserable. When the doors slid shut on us I began tempting him with our options.

"Want to see a movie? They have an octo-plex."

"Seen 'em all already. Twice."

"Matt, look." On each side of the elevator there was a wall chart, behind plexiglass, with little blurbs about various attractions. "Every ninety minutes they sink a pirate ship with real pirates in a sixty-foot-deep lagoon."

"Been there. Done that."

"Oh. What about the *Titanic*? It says here they sink a giant model...blast furnaces spewing fire—"

"We can't go to that, Steph."

"Sure we can! Let's go!" (I thought I'd try relentlessly upbeat again.)

"Read the fine print."

I did.

"Oh."

It turned out that while they sank the fire-spewing model, eighty topless women danced around the spectacle. Restricted.

Now we had arrived on the ground floor. We stepped out.

"Magic show?"

"Nah."

"Virtual-reality video arcade?"

"Nah."

"Matt," I said, unable to keep the exasperation out of my voice, "we're in the most glitzy city in the world. There's got to be *something* you want to do."

I was beginning to get dizzy because ever since we'd hit the ground floor he'd been circling around me, scooter-like, on the damn skateboard.

"Excuse me," a voice said. "You really shouldn't do that in the lobby."

Matt stopped and pressed on the back of the board with his toe and picked it up and put it under his arm again.

"Mister," I said to the man who'd spoken. "Is there anywhere—even a parking lot—where my brother could skateboard for awhile?"

Matt threw me a grateful glance. Here he was surrounded by pirate ships and virtual reality and all he really wanted to do was board for awhile. Something he could do at home almost anywhere.

The man was beaming.

"You mean this dude hasn't checked out the Concrete Powder Park?"

Concrete Powder Park?!

"Get back on the elevator, go two floors down, take the passage with the red stripe over to the wave action pool, then follow the yellow stripe and it'll get you there. No problem."

We were off. Along the red-striped corridor, past the wave action pool, along the yellow stripe past the jungle gyms, past the bumper cars, past the carousel and there it was. Concrete Powder.

I bought myself a magazine and a bag of chips and stretched out on one of the big padded benches that lined the park. Every now and then I'd look up to see Matt—and about fifty other boys just like him—screaming up and over and off enormous ramps and platforms.

So as it turned out, kids were no problem in this place after all. Between the pools and the park and the carousel there had to be a thousand kids down here. A thousand kids whose parents didn't have to worry about them while they gambled away the family savings.

Las Vegas had figured all the angles.

FIFTEEN

We slept late again and checked out of the hotel just on eleven o'clock. Mum and I left our clothes for the ladies who made up the room and Dad gave his blue jacket to a guy who looked like he needed it but, unfortunately, he kept the silver and turquoise tie.

In the taxi on the way to the airport we were all very quiet. There was something strange about seeing Las Vegas in bright daylight. Between the sand of the desert and the completely cloudless sky it was almost too bright. All our eyes, I noticed, were little slits. Through my slits I was watching the road. There was one of those dark patches up ahead that looked wet until you got close to it and it completely disappeared.

"What day is it?" my mum asked. She was in back with me and Matt. Dad was up front with the driver.

"Tuesday," my dad answered. Then, to the driver, "Isn't it?"

It was. I wondered if the driver thought we were just one more dazzled family who'd lost track of time in the artificially lit and misted world of casinos and hotels and amusement parks. I almost felt like telling him that it wasn't Las Vegas that had done this to us at all but the fact that we had changed our lives so that time didn't really matter. At least not the passage of time, anyway, just moments in Time. Tuesday was nothing more substantial than that patch on the road ahead. You could call it whatever you wanted, but it would still disappear before your eyes.

I was very pleased with this thought. I was just about to say it out loud. I was preparing for the nods of understanding from my parents, when my mum looked at her watch and said, "They'll be cashing out about now."

"The afternoon shift's coming on at the plant," my dad said.

"Where you all from?" the driver asked, and then they were into it. The driver had an aunt who lived in Saskatchewan, maybe we knew her? Dad said we'd never been, yet, but who knew? Maybe it was in the cards, so to speak.

Before long the cabby knew all about how we'd discombobulated our lives and were living day to day, going where our moods and little slips of paper took us. The cab driver thought Canadians were just the greatest. Good people. Always came prepared to have a good time and always had it. He and my dad shook hands after he'd pulled our backpacks out of his trunk and put them on the steaming pavement. Three women in track suits nabbed our cab.

It was strange to watch the tourists arriving in their comfortable clothes and sensible shoes and know that in a few hours they'd be caught up in the glittery jittery stream that flowed from boutiques to casinos to shows to boutiques. They were probably blowing a month's salary coming here for a weekend. Even the bank machines dispensed hundred-dollar bills.

"Goodbye, Vegas," my mum said, as the taxi pulled away. Then she pulled out the little red pill box.

We got out of the intense heat and went into the airport and right up to a juice bar. We had decided the night before to do our next choice at the airport. It just made it so much more immediate to be right there and able to take a plane to wherever our next destination might be.

Matt took off his cap and I undid the bandaids and hung them on the counter. They were beginning to lose their stickiness. Mum upended the two wads into the cap and we looked around for someone to do our choosing. We'd had a woman and a man so it seemed only right to have a kid do it. I went over to a man standing at another juice bar with a baby on his hip. The man had no problem with letting his little girl do the choosing and I managed to get the slip out of her hand before she put it in her mouth, but just barely. There was a

little kiddie-spittle on the paper that Mum unfolded and flattened on the counter in front of us.

It was Matt's.

Now I was the only one left without a surprise.

SIXTEEN

I WANT TO SEE THE OLD WOMAN WHO LIVES
IN A SHOE

Now, that was a surprise. To think that Masher-
shredder-boarder-dude Matt wanted to see someone
from Mother Goose. Who would have believed it?

Mum was looking at him with big mushy eyes,
though I'm not sure why, since I was the one who
used to read him his nursery rhymes.

"Oh, Matt," she said, reaching to stroke his head,
which he neatly dodged.

He was digging into his money belt. He pulled
out his wallet. He opened it and seemed to be pok-
ing into the clear plastic pocket for his laminated
identification card, but was in fact sliding out something from behind it.

It was a little three-inch-by-two-inch photograph,
but not at all the sort of typical wallet photo we're all
used to. For one thing, it was in black and white, only
it had aged so much you could really say it was in yellow and brown. It was of a woman with very blonde
hair and dark painted lips, smiling with her head
thrown back and her arms up to her head. There was
a sign behind her that was partly obscured by the

combination of hair and elbows, but to the left of her body we could make out the words: & SHOES.

Matt flipped the little picture over, and there was writing on the back that didn't look familiar to any of us. It said, "The Old Woman Who Lives In A Shoe," and the T, S, L, A and Ws were done with elaborate loopy flourishes.

"Where did you get this, Matt?" Dad asked.

"Gramps."

Even before he said it, we knew it was what he was going to say. I'm not sure how, exactly. Maybe just the age of the picture. And we all knew that the blonde couldn't have been Gram. I'd seen a few pictures of Gram and I couldn't imagine her with her mouth wide open like that. Even in their wedding picture my gramps and she have their lips pressed tight together, though they're smiling.

"He gave this to you?"

"Not exactly."

"What, exactly?"

"It's okay, Matt," Mum said.

And so we heard how Matt used to snoop in Gramps' room, and how Gramps would sit by the hour, reading. And how sometimes, when he read the Bible, he wouldn't turn the pages. So one day when Gramps was out, Matt snuck into his room and took down the Bible and flipped through it and found this picture.

"I looked through that Bible," Dad said. "There was nothing in it."

"I know," Matt said. "I took it the night he died."

Well, I'll be.

"Did he ever talk to you about...this?" Dad asked, tapping the photo.

"Nope."

"Who do you think it is, Gary?"

"An old flame, obviously."

That broke us up—the idea of Gramps having a flame.

"She is kind of a babe," Matt said, and that got us going again. But she *was*. An old-fashioned babe with a smooth wave of hair rolling back and up from her forehead.

"Well, well, well," my dad said when we'd calmed down, and Mum and Matt and I said in unison, "Three more holes in the ground," because that was one of Gramps' expressions.

He had a bunch of expressions that he used over and over again—"You'll never get this hour back" being one of them. Any time you offered him anything—a drink, a cookie, anything—he'd say, "God bless the giving hand." When he finished watching the news on TV he'd say, "It was ever thus." These same expressions, over and over and over again. How are you today? "I'm still here." Care for some coffee? "I won't say no." Well, well, well. "Three more holes in the ground."

"Mind if I hang onto this for awhile, Matt?" Dad asked, picking up the photo.

"Keep it," Matt said. "It's yours, really, sort of. I only stole it."

That got us all laughing again. We were a little punchy.

So it was crazy Matt who finally got us off the North American continent. We all had a guess at what & Shoes meant. Matt and I couldn't think of anything but Socks & Shoes. Mum thought maybe Ladies Wear & Shoes, but Dad thought that the something & Shoes would be a pub somewhere in Scotland because his dad had been stationed in the Orkney Islands when he was a pilot during the war.

"And if that's the case," he said, "it will be something we're not expecting. Not Socks & Shoes but, say, Thistles & Shoes."

"Thistles?"

"Maybe."

"Thistles and shoes? That doesn't go together at all."

"Thistles and bare feet."

"Ooh."

Matt and I didn't even know that Gramps had been in the war.

"Did he kill people?" Matt asked. Mum and I

didn't try to shush him. We were all very curious.

But Dad said he didn't really know much more than that. It seems Gramps was never much of a talker, even before our time. All Dad could remember his father ever saying about the war was "it's over, no point dredging it all up," and "when we flew out of the Orkneys...." These two sentences and a picture of a babe in front of a sign were all we had to go on.

When we landed in Toronto, Mum was wiped. We'd been in the air for hours already and now we were facing another six-hour flight to Scotland. There was an Air Canada flight to Edinburgh in three hours and we could get it a lot cheaper than booking one for the next day because there'd been cancellations. We had a conference.

"C'mon," Dad said. "This'll be good practice for when Steph has us going to Australia."

"Oh, God," my mum said, stretching. "If Steph's making us go to Australia, let's go by boat." She stretched out on a row of uncomfortable-looking seats with her back towards us.

"I think that's a yes, don't you?"

"Go for it, Dad."

While Dad went to buy our tickets and Matt went to the arcade, I headed straight for the ladies' washroom. I was feeling grubby and gungy.

Now that I've become a traveller, I have all sorts of ideas that I would like to see implemented. For instance, there should be big rooms filled with bunks—nothing fancy—that you can rent for even less than a night in a hostel. These should be called Cheap Sleeps, and they should be in airports, bus stations, even those big gas stations along major highways. And there should be coin-operated showers everywhere, too. Nice little moulded jobbies with hand-held showerheads so you can get the water everywhere. When we were on the ferry to Vancouver Island I went into the bathroom and saw a woman bent over one of the sinks washing her hair. At the time I thought this was strange behaviour, but now I understand.

So that's what I did in the ladies' washroom at Pearson International Airport. I washed my hair. One of the bonuses of washing your hair is that it gets your nails really clean. I tidied up carefully after myself so that the other travellers wouldn't have to look at my hair stuck to the sink, and then I proceeded with the rest of me. Water was dribbling down my neck, but some stuff you just have to put up with.

I have perfected the art of getting really clean, body part by body part. I did my feet, one at a time from a standing position. After one foot was washed I dried it with my sock and put on a new sock from my pack. Same with the other foot. Then I washed out my original socks. I would dry them after, under the dryer meant for hands. Face, neck, armpits. And then I brushed my teeth. There's nothing so wonderful after you've been on a plane for hours, and eaten every hard candy or packet of peanuts you could get your hands on, than brushing your teeth.

All I needed now was "scent" as Tanya had called it. I exited the bathroom and started heading for the duty-free shops at the airport. There was one just for booze, one just for munchables, and one just for perfume. There were absolutely huge bottles of perfume in there, the kind you only ever see in magazine ads. Enormous green, amber, pink and blue bottles. Does anyone ever buy those? The stuff in the small bottles was expensive enough.

The only perfume in there was the kind they keep behind locked glass doors in the drugstore. My friends and I could regularly spritz on testers of the other kind without ever incurring more than usual suspicion from the sales clerks. The old "only three students allowed in this store at any time" paranoia. Paranoia? Discrimination.

Anyway, I had just poked my head through the doorway to this store when, immediately, a well-dressed woman stepped up to me.

"May I help you?"

There I was in a T-shirt, carrying an enormous

backpack and with wet hair to boot. I wished Mum was along. But after all this was an airport and I was very, very clean and I *was* wearing fresh socks.

"I'd like to sample some scent, please."

"Certainly," she said, and before I could register amazement at not being treated like a three-only student, she had turned around and was heading for the counter. "What did you have in mind?"

My mind raced. There was no point in trying something I could get by opening up the rub-and-sniff strips in the magazines, so I dredged up something I remembered from an ad that Mum and I had laughed at—the world's costliest perfume.

"Joy," I said. She looked at me. "If you have it."

She reached underneath the counter and lifted up the black atomizer with the red top. I held out my wrist and she spritzed it. I waved it around a bit and then, amazed at myself, said, "I'll want to let it linger."

"Of course."

And I left.

As soon as I was out of sight of the store, I lifted my wrist to my nose. My wrist was still damp from the spray. It's hard to say whether it was wonderful or not, being so expensive it kind of ruined my judgement.

When I got back to Mum, she was still lying down, and Dad and Matt were sprawled nearby. As soon as I joined them, Matt said, "What's that smell?"

"That's Joy," I said.

Mum's eyes opened wide, but she didn't get up.

"The world's costliest perfume?" she said. "Let's smell."

I went over and held my wrist under her nose.

"Mm," she said.

"How much?" the guys wanted to know.

"'One hundred and twenty-five dollars the ounce.'"

"*The* ounce?"

"Yes, *the* ounce."

"Not *an* ounce."

"No, *the* ounce."

"We'll have to buy some," Mum said, closing her eyes again and scrunching even more into her seat, "when Steph has us go to Paris."

"Is Steph sending us to Paris?"

"I thought I was sending us to Australia."

"Then we'll fly out of Paris."

"I thought we were going by boat next time."

"Oh, go to sleep everybody," Mum said, and she did. And not long after, the rest of us did, too.

SEVENTEEN

When it was time to board the plane, we all had neck cricks. A few hours into the flight I was squirming in my seat trying to get comfortable. My legs were all jumpy, and whenever I switched positions they'd get jumpy again in about ten seconds. I tried sitting lotus, I tried curling over on one bum cheek, I tried sitting on my heels. But no matter what I did, the jumpy feeling came back.

At one point in my squirmings, Matt nudged me to look across the aisle at Dad. He was just sitting there staring down at the photo. That's how Gramps must have looked all those nights.

All those nights sitting down in his basement room in our house. All those nights looking at a photo from his past. Had he done that while Gram was still alive? Had he done it every night since the war? Or was it just something he flipped into during his last year?

We'd never know the answer to those questions. A part of me thought we'd never know the answer to a lot of questions.

"Do you think we'll find her?" I asked Matt.

"Sure, yeah," he said. He looked as if it had never

occurred to him that we wouldn't.

"But if she's Gramps' age, she might be dead."

I could tell that thought hadn't occurred to him. After awhile he said, "We'll find & Shoes, anyway."

But I wasn't so sure. I mean, if this was during wartime, maybe the place had got bombed or something. Maybe there was no such thing as & Shoes and hadn't been for more than fifty years. Who would remember it?

But that's not what I said to Matt. I said something worse.

"What if it's just a picture he liked? What if he didn't even know the woman?"

Matt couldn't believe an old geezer like Gramps would carry around a yellowing photo if it didn't mean something to him. But I wasn't really worried that she might have meant nothing to him. In the pit of my stomach I was worried that maybe he might have meant nothing to her.

When we landed at Edinburgh it was raining outside and we were tired and grumpy. In Toronto Dad had actually entertained the idea of renting a car in Scotland to make our way around. But now we had gone through two time changes and it was raining and the prospect of driving on the wrong side of the road with a fried brain was not at all appealing.

We cashed some traveller's cheques at the airport

and put ourselves in the hands of one of the taxi drivers lined up right outside the doors. He said it would only be about twenty minutes to downtown and did we have a hotel? We didn't, of course, and Mum, who sat up front because she had had the most sleep and could at least talk without gobbledygook coming out, asked him if there were any good hostels nearby.

"Och, yes, lass," he said. "Best hostel in all of Scotland's just off the Royal Mile."

He started his meter running, and we headed out in the rain and fog. It was a very good thing Dad had opted out of a car rental because we hit a couple of things they call roundabouts soon after we left the airport and though the taxi driver had no trouble at all, it looked awful. Instead of nice long ramps to merge onto the highway, roundabouts are completely circular sections of road. If you can't squeeze into the correct lane for your particular exit, you could just keep going around and around in circles all day. Add to that the fact that they're all driving on the left instead of the right and it's a nightmare.

Through my own internal traveller's fog of exhaustion I made out Mum's conversation with the driver up front. No, we weren't Americans, we were Canadians, and no, we weren't visiting relatives, we were going to see the Orkney Islands where her father-in-law had been during the war.

"Bless you, dear. Bless the whole lot of you. Navy man, was he?"

When Mum said he was an air man the driver blessed us all again.

"Och, you should've landed at Prestwick," he said. "That's where the RAF was, lass."

I looked over at Matt and Dad to see if they were listening. They were, though they looked pretty out of it. It turned out our taxi driver had an uncle who had worked at Prestwick since it began as a flying field in the 1930s. During the war Britain bought planes from the United States and Canada. Apparently, they got them to Britain by having them flown over instead of packed onto ships. Lots of these planes were flown over by women.

"There was an RAF base near Belfast, what was the end of the Atlantic Air Ferry, see. So planes would go from Canada to Ireland. One day, November 1940 it was, a pilot got lost and landed at Prestwick instead. No one took much notice of 'im—planes were up and down and about all the time—till the man 'imself reported taking off from Gander, Newfoundland. He'd been in the air almost eleven hours!"

"Maybe that was Gramps," Matt said, suddenly a little more alert.

"Bless you, laddie," the driver said. "Bless you."

The driver pointed out a few sights of interest

beyond the rain, but we were really too blown to appreciate them. He waited to see that we'd be able to get into the hostel, then blessed us again as he left us at 8 Blackfriars Street just off the High Street part of the Royal Mile.

We were in hostel heaven. The young guy at reception was really friendly and said there was no problem with checking in now or any time for that matter. This was great, because lots of hostels have very strict rules. At some places you can't check in before four in the afternoon but you have to have checked in by ten or eleven at night. There was no curfew in this hostel, either—not that we cared, we only wanted to sleep—and while the rooms held four to sixteen people, we were lucky enough to be able to get a room with just the four of us. We rolled out our sleeping bags and flopped on the little cots and fell asleep immediately.

EIGHTEEN

I love watching people somehow managing to feed themselves in a communal kitchen without any fights. Or lists. There are never any written rules or specific jobs, and yet somehow everything gets done and cleaned up after, too. It's probably because the kitchen doesn't belong to anyone who's using it. It's like we're all behaving the way we would at a sleep-over. "Don't ask what you can do to help," my mum used to say to me. "Just start helping."

There were lots of people in the hostel—from Japan, Germany, Australia—and they were mostly in their late teens or early twenties. No one was unfriendly, but no one was especially welcoming, either. I sat beside what seemed like a single woman who was reading *The Lonely Planet Guide to Scotland*.

"Hi."

"Hello."

She had an accent.

"My name's Steph."

"What an unusual name."

"Short for Stephanie."

"Ah. I am Marie-Aline," she said, holding out her hand for shaking.

While around us people ate muffins, toast, muesli, and in some cases fried eggs, and talked in a variety of languages, I learned that Marie-Aline was from Paris, that she'd been to Canada a number of times and particularly liked Nova Scotia, which she pronounced Nova Scocha. Apparently, in France, you could get some kind of book of five coupons for five hundred dollars so that once you were in Canada you could fly to any five Canadian destinations for just a hundred dollars a pop.

"So...you could go from B.C. to Newfoundland for just a hundred bucks?"

"That's right. I did that, in fact. And from Newfoundland I took the ferry to Nova Scocha."

Marie-Aline had seen more of Canada than I had. She'd seen more of everywhere. She kept talking about the places she'd been to—Thailand, South America, Alaska—and not just for an overnight stay, either. She'd been in Thailand for almost a year.

"How old are you?" I finally blurted out. "If that's okay to ask."

"It is certainly okay," she said. "I'm forty-one."

"You're older than my mum!"

"Well, I'll be darned."

I loved the way she said darned. Marie-Aline didn't even have a driver's license, and yet she'd been all over the world. She stayed mostly in hostels but carried a tiny pup tent on her backpack. Every now and then she went back to Paris to earn a little money and see her mother and then she took off again. She'd started travelling like this when she was sixteen.

"Sixteen?"

"Yes."

"On your own?"

"Yes."

"Weren't you scared?"

She was looking at me but not answering. I knew the word for scared in French was *peur* and I was about to say it when she leaned in towards me.

"I will tell you my method. I would arrive in an unfamiliar town and I would pick the bar that had the best music. I would go up to the bartender—always the old ones, never the young—and somehow communicate to him a desire to wash glasses." Here she mimed wiping. "This they were always happy to have me do. And they looked out for me. So. When the bar closed, in exchange for my work"—she mimed wiping again—"I would sleep safe and sound on the floor of the bar. I had clean washrooms, a safe, locked-up place to stay, and I could sleep late because bars don't open until the afternoon in any case."

Marie-Aline spoke French, English and Spanish perfectly and German and Italian imperfectly. I bet her idea of imperfect was my idea of great.

"I kept my wits about me, you see, Steph," she said, getting up to do her dishes. "I still do."

We talked for another ten or fifteen minutes and she gave me a bunch of other tips. She knew more about travelling than anyone I'd ever met.

When Mum and Dad and Matt emerged and I made introductions and more people heard that we were going to the Orkneys, there were all kinds of offers of advice.

"Go from Scrabster—"

"Go from John O'Groats—"

"Get the kids a Student Rail Card—"

"Too expensive, go by bus—"

"National Express—"

"Citylink's better—"

"Get the Go Blue Banana minibus."

That last appealed, of course, to Matt and me, but it turned out not to link up to Scrabster or John O'Groats but was a hop-on, hop-off tour that led back to Edinburgh. The bus completed a circuit every day, stopping at hostels and campsites if they were given advance notice. And once you bought a ticket, there was no time limit, so you could get on in Edinburgh, hop off at Loch Ness, say, see the monster and stay there for months before hoping on and off again. Marie-Aline, of course, had already done it, but she'd taken the Haggis Backpackers minibus.

"Uh, oh," my mum said. "I think we're going to have to do a few things before Australia."

I didn't say it, but as appealing as I found the Go Blue Banana minibus, I just couldn't see doing it as a family. By the time we'd all agreed where to hop off, the town would have gone by. And by the time we'd decided where to hop on, the bus would have gone by. As it was, once we'd ventured outside and walked up to the Royal Mile—a street that ended with a view of Edinburgh Castle—we couldn't agree on our next course of action at all.

At a place that sold newspapers we bought something called *The List*, because it listed all the pubs in Edinburgh, and while there was nothing on there that ended in & Shoes, there were such great names, like Sneeky Pete's and The Laughing Duck, that it made us want to go to a pub. We chose one and got completely turned around and bummed out trying to find it. So, even though we'd passed tons of pubs trying to find a pub, we just suddenly turned off at the first sign that said Fish 'n' Chips and went in.

Everybody was grumpy. We all ordered fish 'n' chips without even looking at the menu, and Dad ordered a glass of beer with his. When Mum looked at him funny he said, "Make that a pint of stout." When a coffee-and-donut man starts swilling stout before noon, you know he's tense.

There was a long silence while we all looked at

whatever pamphlet or flyer we could pull out of our various zippered compartments. Matt and I pretended to study *The List*.

"I don't know why men are so stupid about getting lost," Mum finally said. So in a way, she started it.

"Don't call me stupid." Pause. "And we're not lost."

"All right." Pause. "Okay." Pause. "I'm sorry I called you stupid." Breath. "But how can you say we're not lost?"

"We know where we are. We're in Scotland, we're in Edinburgh, we're at—"

"Oh, this again. This line of reasoning. I suppose we can never be lost because we're on planet Earth."

Pause.

"Lost is not knowing where you are."

Pause.

"Lost is not knowing how to get to where you want to go."

"But we don't really know yet where it is we want to go."

"Well, when we do, we won't know how to get there. So we're lost."

It was like they were speaking two different languages. When they finally appealed to us kids—we were poring over the list of pubs—I tended to agree with Dad and Matt with Mum, so it wasn't a gender thing after all.

I think the impossibility of our task was beginning to become apparent. Sitting around an airport, the idea of tracking down & Shoes was intriguing. It was all theoretical and we could all fantasize about how it would go smoothly and turn out perfectly. But the reality of finding ourselves in huge unfamiliar cities with no clear goal came crashing in.

We ate our fish 'n' chips in silence.

Though it had been a girl who had served us, there was an old man operating the cash register as we were leaving and, on hearing our accents, he naturally wanted to chat. We were in no mood. Dad briefly told him our story and his eyes lit up. For the fourth or fifth time since hitting Edinburgh we were blessed.

"Is there a list like this for the Orkneys?" Matt asked, holding up *The List*.

"Shouldn't think so, no," he said, but he was obviously interested, so Matt started telling him about & Shoes. Mum and Dad and I were trying to inch our way out when we heard the word Internet.

Internet?

The old guy told the girl to keep an eye on things and he beckoned us into the back room. There, just to the left of the deep-fryers, was a computer, a starburst screen-saver pattern shifting around on the colour monitor.

"Me son-in-law gave me this," he said, tapping

with two fingers on the keyboard. "She's got 8 megabytes of RAM and a 1.1 gigabyte hard drive."

Mum and Dad and Matt and I looked at each other over his bald head as he punched away. It was bad enough that this old guy's system, in the back of an old restaurant beside his old grill, made ours at home look like a fossil. What was worse was that we hadn't even thought of it. We looked a little sheepish as he got on-line. After a moment he told us there were sixty thousand pubs in the British Isles and he could download them all. We thought that wouldn't be necessary.

"Sixty thousand? Won't that take forever?" Mum asked.

"Well, it's in the Orkneys, you say, so we'll do a search there, you see."

He keyed in Orkneys. Nothing. Then Scotland. Likewise nothing. But, undaunted, he kept going. All sorts of &s started to appear on screen. Axe & Compasses. Bull & Swan. Butt & Oyster.

"Bingo," he said.

We all leaned in to look at the screen. There it was. Elephant & Shoes. We were not only in the wrong city, we were in the wrong country.

The Elephant & Shoes was in London, England.

NINETEEN

Even Mum didn't push for seeing the sights in Edinburgh before heading to London. We were hot on the chase. There really was a pub called Elephant & Shoes and it hadn't been bombed to smithereens. It still existed.

The old guy, whose name was Craig MacDonald, was apologetic that he couldn't book our train to London right from his 486. Travel arrangements on the World Wide Web, he said, weren't as efficient as people might think. When Mum and Dad mumbled something about reimbursing him for his time and trouble, he wouldn't hear of it.

"Och, no," he said. "Me son-in-law's payin' fer it all this first year anyway. Compuserv. Travelnet. The works."

He even printed out little maps and itineraries for us. One of these was a map of Edinburgh on which he marked, with a red pencil, our route from his fish 'n' chip shop back to the High Street Hostel.

There was a laundry service at this hostel, so we forked over a couple of pounds for that. And once again we took everything out of our packs and re-packed them.

Marie-Aline and all the others were gone. I knew they wouldn't be back because the cots where they had slept the night before already had different packs and books thrown on top of them to save them. I felt a little pang of regret that I wouldn't see her again.

We hung around the hostel that evening flopped on our cots and read about all the sights we wouldn't be seeing in the guidebooks that were piled up everywhere. Mr. MacDonald had made a number of suggestions, of course. He thought that we should at least see a few sights, on our way, so he pushed for something called The Slow Coach. It's a bus that does a big loop from London in England to Edinburgh in Scotland and takes in all kinds of places like Stratford-upon-Avon and Bath. And, like the Go Blue Banana, you can hop on and hop off and take two months to do your loop. Or, if you decide to stay in one place along the way, you can sell the rest of your ticket. It blew me away that trains and buses were set up for people to mosey about here, whereas in Canada everything seemed to be set up for the nine-to-five crowd.

"Population," Mum said. "Twice Canada's."

It was hard to get your head around. And the whole country would fit into one of our Great Lakes. How could such a small place be so big?

Next morning, when we went to check out, we

stopped at the counter but there was no one there. At least, there didn't seem to be anyone there. When we peered over the counter there was a woman—she had to be at least fifteen years older than my mum—down on her knees staring at what seemed to be a bunch of squares of different pieces of coloured cloth. My dad was about to slap the little bell, but my mum stopped him. Instead, she went through the swinging half door to the other side of the counter and we all trooped in after her. In addition to the woman and the scraps of cloth, there were bags and bags of what looked like kids' clothes and old dresses and blouses.

"Oh," the woman said, looking up finally, "you gave me a start. So sorry."

She began to stand up, but my mum stopped her with a hand on the woman's shoulder.

"May I ask what you're doing?" Mum asked.

"'Course, dear," the woman said. "I'm quiltin'."

My mum looked from the woman back to the colourful squares on the bare linoleum floor. There was no evidence of that white stuff that goes inside a quilt. There was no sewing machine behind the desk, no pieces of ribbon. I suppose if I'd been very observant I'd have noticed, before the woman pointed it out, a single pincushion in the shape of a tomato with a couple of needles in it. But all we could see was a bunch of little squares—some shiny, some patterned, some plain—arranged in no apparent order.

"I like this piece," she said, meaning the orange-and-blue bit of cloth in her right hand, "but I can't see where it should go."

To my amazement, my mum reached out and put her finger next to a piece of material with a zig-zag pattern on it. There was a few seconds of silence before the woman said, "Hm," and tried placing the square where my mum had suggested.

"By George, dear," she said, "I think you've got it."

Then she started rearranging, quickly, almost in a bit of a frenzy, some of her other squares that she'd already placed, and then they sat back and looked at the new arrangement together. They were both nodding slowly at this new configuration, when the woman snapped out of it and stood up.

"Well, I expect you want to be on your way."

We *were* on a mission, but my mum wanted to see a finished quilt. The woman went to a big cupboard at the end of the room where extra linens and pillows were stored, and she pulled out a big folded square of material. When she unrolled it for us all to see, even Matt was impressed.

"Cool," he said, and the woman beamed.

It was cool. It was such a conglomeration of different colours, but when you looked closely, each section that you thought was one colour only was actually made up of about ten little pieces of a similar colour. Some parts of the quilt seemed to pop out and some to recede. My mum asked the woman how much she sold them for and she laughed. Who could afford to pay what they were worth? Thousands of hours went into each one.

"I keep those I can't part with," she said, nodding her head, "like this here. And others I give away. Everyone knows what they're going to get from me these days...especially those as have had a new babby."

She folded the quilt again and stepped over the pieces on the floor and we checked out. When we looked back there was no one at the counter, and we knew she was already back on her knees, contemplating her scraps of coloured cloth.

Instead of taking two months on a slow coach, or even a couple of days, we got the fastest train we could. It was called the Flying Scotsman, and it made the almost four-hundred-mile trip from Edinburgh to London in four hours.

Londoners weren't quite as friendly as Edinburghers, or whatever they're called. At least not the ones we met. No one blessed us. We made our way to our hotel, which was called the Hansel & Gretel. Matt and I, naturally, expected a little thatched cottage in the woods or something, but of course this was in the middle of London, and it was a huge white painted brick building with all kinds of white painted fire escapes up and down the walls, even at the front. Mr. MacDonald had been able to tell us in advance that the hostels were all full, which shows how many people there were because there were lots of hostels in London.

Anyway, when we paid the taxi driver who let us off, without blessing us, and went into the Hansel & Gretel and found our rooms, they were...down. I mean down. Down, down, we went even from street level. Down, down to a room that was pretty much like the hostel room, only much less sunny and much more expensive. In fact, Dad and Matt took the room that had no window and Mum and I took the one with a tiny window that looked out onto concrete about a foot and a half away. Looking out and up, we could see people moving around on the street level. It was weird.

We invited the guys into our room for a conference.

"I'm starved."

"Me, too."

"I think we should find the Elephant & Shoes first, then eat."

"I think we should eat first, then find the Elephant & Shoes."

"Why don't we eat at the Elephant & Shoes?"

Everywhere else we'd been, simply standing in

one place and looking pathetic was enough to get people asking if they could help us out. Not here. We were passed by in droves. People went out of their way to avoid meeting our eyes. In desperation, we piled into a taxi.

"The Elephant & Shoes, please," Dad said, getting into the front seat, and before he could say the address, the driver cut him off.

"I know it well enough," he said.

We sat there in silence for about three and a half minutes while the driver did a turn here, a jog there and pulled over to the curb in front of a pub. My dad handed over what didn't amount to much more than the minimum fare, plus a tip, and the driver took it, said, "Right then," and did a strange movement with his head.

"Did he say, 'Be off'?" my mum asked.

She was still looking at the taxi cab pulling away.

"No, Elly."

"He did. He said, 'Be off.'"

"He said, 'See ya,'" Matt said.

Matt and I were standing there amazed by the sign in front of us: Elephant & Shoes. It was exactly like the sign in Gramps' picture. A perfect match. Only now that we had it in front of us in living colour, we could see that the sign was carved out of wood and the raised letters were painted white.

"I should have got his license number," Mum

113

said. "What was the cab company, Gary?"

"I don't know, Elly. Look."

The pub in front of us just a few feet across the sidewalk was big—three storeys of old stone. There were carved wood panels over the door that looked older and a lot more elaborate than the sign itself did. There were lions and trees and stuff carved on them. Above the wood panels were glass windows, but standing a few inches out from the glass was a grid of black iron. The horizontal ribs of each grid went right into the stone, and the vertical ribs ended in points beneath a stone arch.

"It's like Victoria times ten," Matt said.

"Times ten."

No one moved.

"We ought to go in."

"Of course we're going in."

"This is why we came here."

"This is why, all right."

"I just want to look at it awhile."

"Me, too."

"Me, too."

"I'll write an open letter to all the cab companies—"

"Mum?" Matt said. "Let it go."

Mum pressed her lips together.

"Fine," she said. And she went towards the big heavy door of the Elephant & Shoes. When we all followed, we found Mum just standing inside the inner doorway, looking.

"It's so beautiful," she whispered, as though we were in a library.

And it was beautiful. There were wooden barrels behind the bar with brass faucets sticking out of them. The barrels themselves, and all the booze bottles and glasses, were in individual arched alcoves a few feet deep. The bar was solid wood and had flowers and loops carved into it and the bar top was solid marble about three inches thick. Every pillar in the place, from the large ceiling-to-floor ones to the small ones that jutted out at the end of the bar, was carved with knobs and curls. Even the ceiling was carved with an enormous repeating pattern of spirals and leaves.

A burst of laughter from some men around the bar broke our spell and we took a booth. We weren't sure what the routine was in a pub. Were we supposed to go up to the bar and get our food? Was a waitress going to come and serve us? There was a blackboard menu hanging from various spots on the walls with items like Cornish pasty, sausages, and something called a ploughman's lunch. Just about everything except the ploughman's lunch seemed to come with chips and beans. Painted on the bottom of the blackboard were the words: Nothing to Eat But Food.

"I don't get it."

"Me, neither."

"British humour."

"I guess."

Eventually, a waitress with fluffy bright red hair did come over to us and took our orders without writing them down. Even though she was really busy she was very smiley and friendly. She had a gap between her front teeth, called my mum "Ducks" and made up for the surly cab driver in no time flat.

Mum and I had the ploughman's lunch, which is basically hunks of different kinds of cheese and pickles and thick slices of bread. Dad had lamb curry with rice, and Matt had the jumbo sausages with chips and beans. This time both Mum and Dad had beer in a big glass mug with about an inch of foam on top. Our waitress got it by pulling on a big white handle with a round black sign on it that we could read even from where we were sitting: The Genuine Webster's Yorkshire Bitter Brewed in the Pennines. Matt tried Dad's and I tried Mum's and it was definitely bitter.

We were having fun. Mum asked the waitress on one of her fly-bys if anyone famous had dined here and she said, "Cor, ducks. Dickens, Johnson, Thackeray...Virginia Woolf an' that lot. Oo 'asn't?"

Then she was off again.

"Dickens," Matt said. "The Scrooge guy?"

"The Scrooge guy."

But what was really interesting was that Gramps had been here. We tried to imagine him, and it, fifty years or more ago.

"Maybe he sat right here," Matt said.

"Maybe he did."

But what he probably did most of the time was stand around the bar like so many men and women were doing right then. There was a brass rail all around the bottom of the bar about six inches off the ground for people to rest their feet on. I tried to imagine Gramps, in a uniform, standing there with a pint of bitter in his hand and his foot up on the railing. It wasn't easy.

Everything the four of us knew about England came from TV. Mum's family was originally from the States and Dad's, way back, was from Ireland. It was weird to be in a place that was so old, where every time you turned a corner there was a little plaque naming who had lived and worked there...four hundred years ago. We knew a lot about Charles and Di but practically nothing about anything else. Now that I'd actually been there, I found it interesting. Of course, even Las Vegas was more interesting to me now that I'd actually been there. I could just imagine how interested Marie-Aline would be in current events, considering she'd been just about everywhere.

We didn't want to leave the Elephant & Shoes, ever, but we'd finished our lunch and since it was a busy place we felt too guilty to take up space. My dad, emboldened by his Yorkshire Bitter, took the yellowing picture out of his wallet and showed it to our waitress behind the bar. She looked at it. Then she looked at it again. Then her eyes widened and she grinned her gap-toothed grin. Was she just smiling at the old picture of & Shoes? Mum and Matt and I slid out of our booth and went up to the bar, too.

She did recognize her.

"Cor, yes, it's Mrs. Pigott! Me Uncle Tim bought this place off 'er."

Then came the big question.

"Is she still alive?"

"I'd say so, yeh. Still comes to London now and again and still drops in 'ere."

Still comes to London. Where was she?

"Eelee," the waitress said, which turned out to be spelled Ely, just one L short of Mum's name, which we all took to be A Sign.

We didn't want to take up too much of the waitress's time, but she said it was no bother and told us to go to Victoria Station, look for trains to Norwich (she pronounced it like porridge—Norridge) and 'op off at Eelee.

"Say 'ullo to the old duck for us, will yer?"

118

Now we had a decision. Should we go back to the Hansel & Gretel and get our backpacks and stay in Ely when we got there? We decided no. We decided that finding our way to wherever Mrs. Pigott—it was so weird to have a name for her—was, would be stressful enough. We decided to poke around London for a day until we were tired, then leave by an early train the next day. That way we could travel without all our packs and junk.

TWENTY

My mum and I both had trouble sleeping that night. Maybe it was partly the sub-sidewalk room, but I think mostly it was excitement. We tried counting backwards, first from a hundred, then two hundred and finally five hundred. Just when I thought she was asleep for real and I was the only wide-awake person in the whole world, I heard *tsssss*.

"What? What?"

"I thought we'd be going to Disney World next," she said.

"Florida or California?"

"Euro-Disney."

"Well, we still could if you want."

"No, thank you."

Long pause.

"You still awake, Mum?"

"Yup."

"You think she'll remember him?"

"I've been wondering about that. I don't know. It's amazing enough that she's alive and we've found her, isn't it?"

"Yeah."

Except it wasn't. I wanted her to remember him.

"I'm so proud of Matt."

"Yeah."

"I'm going to count again."

"Okay."

After another long pause, I asked Mum if she was awake and this time there was no answer. I thought she might be kidding until I heard her breathing. I rolled onto my stomach and put the pillow over my head.

The next thing I knew, Mum's wristwatch was making its tiny alarm noise. We had agreed to wake the guys, who were in total darkness.

Breakfast at the hotel was at ground level but strange. The toast was brought after we'd finished our eggs and sausage, and the triangular slices were lined up in something that looked like a tiny desk organizer. It was previously warmed white bread more than it was toast. It was cold.

We all wanted to look our best for Mrs. Pigott, and so Dad thought he should wear his western-style tie. Even Mum said no to this. Matt had packed a T-shirt that didn't have anything written on it and so that's what he wore. Mum had a short-sleeved blouse with a collar, and I put on a black tank top I have with a little lace insert at the V of the neck. Dad ended up wearing his light collarless shirt with thin blue stripes. We looked so nicely unencumbered with just our money belts.

Victoria Station was confusing, but we managed. Again we were impressed by the amount of countryside in England. We passed field after field, very flat and divided into irregular shapes by stone walls or hedges. And the rivers were raised up in embankments like they'd been planned. We pretty much kept our noses to the window the whole way, but Mum and Dad were especially gawky when we stopped in Cambridge.

"That's it. Isn't it? That must be it."

"Which ones?"

"All of them."

They were pointing to the tops of very old buildings they thought would be Cambridge University, where Mr. Chips was. Like I said, all we knew about England came from TV. We didn't see anybody on bicycles wearing graduation gowns, but then it was summertime.

As the train pulled out of Cambridge, pop. 100,000, Dad said, "Or was it Oxford?"

And then, before we knew it, we were in Ely.

A lot of people got off the train. We stopped to read a plaque that said some saint, years ago, turned the local monks into eels because he didn't feel they were religious enough. Nice guy. Anyway, that's how it got the name Ely.

We got directions to the tourist information place. Leave the station—on a street called, appropriately enough, Station Road—and stay on that till you hit Back Hill, which becomes The Gallery. The tourist office was in a place called Cromwell House, and everybody was very helpful. They wanted us to take a tour of their town and cathedral, which was right next door, and we said of course, then took the free maps over to the telephone.

There was only one Pigott in Ely. Bingo, as Mr. MacDonald would say.

My dad wrote down her address and we went back to the information desk and, for a few cents, or pence, as they say, we had a pamphlet called *Town Walks*. *Town Walks* really wanted us to take in all the old buildings, beginning with the cathedral. When we went by it, Matt read out, "'Brass-rubbing centre: free admission.' Who wants to rub their brass?"

We tried to explain that it wasn't rubbing their brass, it was brass-rubbing. He didn't get it until I reminded him that we used to do it all the time.

"We did?"

"Sure. Put a piece of paper over a penny, right? And rubbed with a pencil till the maple leaf design came up."

He was impressed, I think, that something we used to do as kids was considered worth doing by tourists.

All of this chatter was probably just a way of covering our nervousness over The Visit. When we found ourselves in front of Mrs. A. Pigott's address, it wasn't at all old or spectacular like the centre of town. We had all imagined her in a little thatched cottage or something. I believe my own inner picture of her house was based largely on the dwarfs' home in Snow White. And why not? There really were houses with thatched roofs here, and we'd seen them from the train. Everything was so old. Everywhere we turned, there were cobblestones and ivy and chimney pots. Lots and lots of chimney pots that looked very much like long inverted versions of red clay flower pots, sticking up out of the roofs of houses.

But the building we were looking at now was a three-storey rectangular red brick building. Straight up and down. No ivy. No chimney pots. A seniors' apartment complex.

There were old ducks, and whatever the male equivalents of old ducks are, sitting about in lawn chairs out front. More women than men. We walked up the cement pathway and pushed the button that said Pigott.

Tsssss.

There was no answer.

"Maybe she's deaf."

"We should have phoned first."

"If she's deaf it wouldn't make any difference."

Another push of the button and again no answer.

"We should have brought her something!"

Just as we were feeling like uncouth people for not bringing something for our visit with an old lady, a woman who looked about sixty appeared at the locked glass door. She opened it and poked her head through.

"May I help you?"

"We're looking for Mrs. Pigott."

"Anne? I believe she's in. Step in, won't you?"

We stepped into the lobby of this place which was very modern with pale wood chairs and big glass windows. We could see through to the men and women sitting out front.

"My name's Grace Bentley. I'm the super."

"How do you do?" my mum said. I'd never heard her say how do you do in my life.

"How d'you do," Grace said back.

She went to a door on the first floor and rapped loudly. No answer. She called out, "Anne? Anne, it's me, Grace." Still no answer. She was pulling some keys out of her pocket and was just about to try them on the doorknob when an old woman poked her head out of one of the other doors.

"Gone shoppin'," she said, and disappeared again.

"Thank you, Myra," Grace said to the closed door. Then to us, "Would you like to wait? I can't imagine she'll be too long...unless she's at a matinee."

We followed Grace back out to the lobby and sat in the pale wood chairs. We said no we didn't need tea but thank you, and she went back into her own apartment.

"Mum," Matt said. "When someone says how do you do, shouldn't you say fine thanks?"

"No, that's if they say how are you. If they say how do you do, you say how do you do right back."

"Like good day and good day."

"Exactly."

"How d'yew dew?"

"Howdydoo?"

Through the big windows we saw an old woman coming along the sidewalk. She had on a navy blue straw hat with flowers on the rim and, like so many of the people on the front lawn, she was wearing a sweater even though it wasn't cold out. Under the sweater was a pink blouse and a navy blue skirt that fell to just below her knees. Her shoes were navy blue slip-ons. In each hand she carried a shopping bag. She was very thin. She paused to say something to one of the women on the lawn and then she came in through the first set of doors. My dad was immediately on his feet and opening the second set of doors before she had to find her key.

"Thank you," she said. Then she started down the hallway. We were all a little stunned. Was she the one?

TWENTY-ONE

"Mrs. Pigott?" my dad said.

She stopped and turned around.

"Ye-es?" She pulled her shoulders up when she said that. Her face looked nothing like The Babe. It looked wizened. "Do I know you?" she asked.

We were all having our own thoughts. Dad was thinking we'd handled this badly, we should have called. Mum was thinking we should have brought her something—flowers or sweets. I was thinking what if she had a heart attack, and Matt was thinking, "She's so old."

"Let me help you with those," my dad finally said, but she hung on to her shopping bags with an iron grip. She stared him down.

"I'm sorry," he said. "Let me introduce myself. And my family."

We all got up on cue and went over to them. By the time we'd done our how d'you dos, it was clear she still didn't have a clue who we were or why we were there.

Then Dad said, "I'm Dan's son—Dan Shaw," and a little light went on in her eyes.

"Good heavens," she said.

And then she smiled. An enormous face-splitting smile with beautiful pearly-white teeth. It was The Babe, more than half a century later. She put down the two shopping bags and shook hands all round, and we all did another round of how d'you dos.

"You must come in," she said, bending to pick up her bags, but Dad and Matt beat her to it. And so we followed her down the hall, Mum quietly *tsssssing*.

The door opened into the tiniest apartment I'd ever seen. It was pretty much just one room with a kitchenette on one side and a bathroom and bedroom on the other. Through the open door of the small bathroom I could see that the tub had one of those handle things we'd put in our house for Gramps, plus a longer one on the wall, which he hadn't had. In fact the entire hallway of the apartment complex had railings on each side for the old folks to hang on to as they made their way to their rooms. Mrs. Pigott hadn't needed to do that.

In the living room there were a couple of big old chairs with a small table between them. Each chair had a footstool with roses embroidered on it. In the kitchenette there was a small oval-shaped glass table with two wrought-iron chairs, one on either side. The opposite wall to the door we had come in was almost entirely made up of sliding glass doors. Through these we could see, just to the side of the doors, the tiniest patch of garden with tall spiky flowers growing out of it.

Mrs. Pigott took the navy blue straw handbag, which perfectly matched her hat, from her right arm and put it on top of the little fridge.

"You can just put those on the table if you'd be so kind," she said to Dad and Matt about the shopping bags. Those two bags pretty much took up the entire space on the tabletop. "I'll put on tea, shall I?" to which we all responded simultaneously that we would love some tea. We were a little nervous.

Then she took off her straw hat and as she was placing it on top of the matching handbag I couldn't help noticing how much hair she had, and how perfectly white it was. She fluffed it a little, to get rid of the ridge created by the hat, and her arms were up in almost the same pose as they had been in the picture. Except this time her head wasn't thrown back.

She plugged in the kettle. She warmed the pot. She took out a couple of plates, then reached into her shopping bag and started undoing packages and arranging the contents on the plates.

"May I help?" my mum asked, to which Mrs. Pigott naturally said, "I'm quite all right, thank you."

Mum seemed to realize immediately that she'd broken her own sleepover rule, and so she started arranging seating. Mrs. Pigott should have a big chair and so should Dad. She brought the two little wrought-iron ones in from the kitchen for me and her and pulled one of the footstools away from the chairs for Matt. He didn't like that much, but if he'd tried sitting on the padded vinyl of one of those tiny wrought-iron numbers for very long, I think he'd have realized that he got the better end of the deal.

"Have you seen the Ship of Fens?" Mrs. Pigott asked, while she waited for the tea to boil.

We hadn't seen any ships at all, but she explained that Ship of Fens was the nickname for the cathedral.

"There's some fine brass in there," Matt said. Mum's and Dad's and my eyeballs flitted back and forth at that one.

"Ye-es," Mrs. Pigott said. "The masks are a little macabre, though, aren't they?"

"Yeah," Matt said. I don't think he even knew what macabre meant. He was the only one who seemed to be at all relaxed, and he wasn't faking it. "Why is it called the Ship of Fens again?"

"Oh, well," she said, getting down a tea pot. "Ely used to be an island, of course."

"Really?"

"Yes, they didn't drain the fens until the seventeenth century."

The way she spoke was so neat. "Century" was "senshreh." So that explained the water running in embankments around the fields. We were on a swamp.

"Those are lupins, aren't they?" Matt asked, pointing to the spiky flowers outside the glass doors.

"Yes," Mrs. Pigott said, and before Mum and Dad and I had time to eyebeam each other again, Matt and Mrs. Pigott were in a discussion about how even the tiny garden she was able to have in this apartment was a real treat.

My dad took the tray with the tea pot and cups and milk and sugar on it, and I got the two plates with the cookies. Mrs. Pigott sat in one of the big chairs. The leftover footstool was used to hold the cookies. The tray was put on the table between the two chairs, after Mrs. Pigott had shoved an ashtray and what looked like a little makeup bag aside.

"Would anyone care to join me?" she said, undoing the clasp of the little bag and pulling out a cigarette.

No one did. She didn't apologize for smoking or ask if anyone minded. Dad struck one of the matches for her and she leaned in and lit her cigarette. She inhaled deeply so that her nostrils pressed in, and then she blew out the smoke in a steady stream.

"Well, well, well," she said.

We didn't say it.

She sat very straight with her left arm crossed in front of her and the elbow of her right arm, the one that held the cigarette, resting on it.

"Let me be sure I have your names," she said. She turned to my dad. "Gary." Then she went counter-clockwise around the little room, slowly. "Matt. Sss...Stephanie. And Elly." As she said each of our names she looked right into our eyes. Then she said, "And I'm Anne."

No one said anything while she tapped the end of her cigarette on the side of her ashtray and a lit-tle cylinder of grey ash fell off. Everything she did, she did slowly. When her elbow was back resting on her crossed arm, Matt spoke up.

"How old are you, Anne?"

The rest of us thought he'd insulted a British lady, but she beamed her big smile again and answered him. Matt looked over at me. She was five years older than Gramps. She looked like she could last a lot longer, too, especially going at that speed.

"Now you tell me," she said. "How is Danny?"

We hadn't thought of that.

"He's dead," my dad said, quickly, to get it over with. There was just a little pause before she replied, "I'm so sorry." But she was saying she was sorry to us, for us, not for her.

My mum started in then with how we were trav-elling as a family and how we'd gone to British Columbia and Las Vegas. I felt she was going on a bit, but Anne seemed to be enjoying it. When Mum finally wound down she said, "It sounds perfectly lovely."

"It was Matt who wanted to meet you."

There was a long pause.

"Matt, was it?"

"Yeah," Matt said. "Show her the picture, Dad."

My dad took the picture out of his wallet and handed it to Mrs. Pigott. She looked down at it for a long time before lifting her head with that big grin. "Wasn't I the cat's pyjamas?"

We all laughed.

"Your hair was so blonde," I said.

"Dyed."

"Really?"

"Oh, yes. I was everything in those days, before the war, especially—blonde, brunette, redhead. I even tried jet black at one point." She handed the photo back to Dad. "I used to touch up my roots with a toothbrush and peroxide. Drove my genuinely blonde girlfriends to distraction."

"Cool," Matt said.

"Quite," she said, squashing her cigarette stub into the ashtray. "If I were a young woman today, I think I'd have pink or blue hair."

"And a nose ring?" Matt asked.

"Several. And tattoos."

We all laughed and relaxed a bit more. As I looked over at Mrs. Pigott, she seemed a lot less wizened than when we'd first seen her. She still had lots of wrinkles and everything, but her whole face looked softer, especially when she smiled. She didn't just smile with her mouth but with her eyes, too.

Mum put on a second pot of tea. Anne excused herself, slowly and carefully, to go to the "W.C." We whispered a few things to each other and then she was in her chair again, leaning back and getting straight to the point.

"I can't tell you much about your grampa," she said to Matt and me. "I didn't know him all that well."

"What kind of plane did he fly?" Matt asked. It wasn't a question that would have entered my head.

"A Mosquito."

Dad said that was more than he knew about his father. At least from those days. I noticed she said it without thinking very hard.

"Did you live in The Shoes?"

"Oh, yes," she said. "My mother ran the place as a boarding-house—there are rooms upstairs. I never had much to do with it. You see, my mother wanted me to be a lady, and so she sent me away to school. I saw very little of her when I was a child." There was a long pause. "She was what you would call nowadays a single mum."

"But the waitress said you ran the pub, that they bought it off you."

"Yes. You see, I came home when war broke out. Worked alongside Mum—" Here she went into a story about how everyone loved her mother. How she was a "character" and always wore a funny hat. How, even for years after the war was over, the ones who had survived came back to the Elephant & Shoes and wanted to see her just as she was so she kept wearing the hat. "And then, when she went downhill, my husband and I took it over."

"Why was it called the Elephant & Shoes?"

"Cockney rhyming slang."

"What's that?" Matt asked.

"Well, instead of saying the word, you give a rhyme for it. Skin and blister, that's your sister. Brass tacks, those are the facts."

She gave a few more examples, and then we started playing a game. We'd give her a word—money, for instance—and she'd give us the rhyming slang for it: bees and honey.

"Wife," said Dad.

"Ooh...struggle and strife."

Even Mum laughed at that one.

"Butter," I said.

"Mutter 'n' stutter."

As she sipped her tea, Mrs. Pigott explained that the rhymes were often shortened so that the rhyme got lost. People would say, "Use your loaf," meaning use your head—loaf of bread. Bread rhymes

135

with head, but they say loaf. When we got that one, she gave us another. "Don't forget yer titfer," meaning hat. Tit for tat rhymes with hat, but they say titfer.

"It makes it very confusing for people who aren't Cockney," said Mum.

"Part of the point, I think."

"What does Elephant & Shoes mean?" I asked.

"Elephant's trunk means you're drunk. Bottles of booze that's your shoes."

So the meaning of & Shoes, the mystery that had led us here, was solved.

"Oh, The Shoes was quite the hang-out then," she said. "Especially for the Americans and Canadians. Jerry Wilmot used to be a great regular and favourite."

We all looked at her with completely blank faces.

"Oh. He was a radio personality during wartime. Canadian. David Niven was about a good deal—"

"The movie star?" my dad asked.

"That's right. It was a pretty lively crowd then."

Where did Gramps fit in, I wondered. Where did Gramps fit in among the fast-talking movie and radio stars? Did he sit there with his lips pressed together, disapproving of them all?

"Did you know Billy Bishop?" Matt asked, and before the rest of us had a chance to roll our eyes at him, Mrs. Pigott handled it gracefully.

"Different war, I'm afraid. I should like to have known him."

And then she pulled another cigarette out of its case and started talking almost as if we weren't there. It was like she was remembering stuff and thinking out loud.

"In those days, well, there was no way a British soldier would push a baby pram, for instance. But the Americans and Canadians were very different. A young mother might be struggling with a pram and perhaps a package or two, and before she knew it she would be flanked by a couple of American service-men. One would take over the packages and the other would happily push the pram. We'd never seen anything like it. They were exuberant." There was a pause. "Our boys didn't care for it very much."

She took a puff on her cigarette, then placed it in the ashtray and slowly stood, pushing herself up against the arms of the chair.

"I think she must be tiring," Mum whispered when she had disappeared into the tiny bedroom next to the bathroom. "We should go soon."

We all knew we should, but we didn't want to.

"Maybe we should take her out to dinner," Dad whispered back.

"Yeah!" Matt and I agreed.

She came slowly back, and after she had lowered herself into her chair, she looked over at my dad.

"There," she said. "You may have that."

It was a small heart-shaped piece of clear plastic about an inch and a half high, with a maple leaf stuck in the middle. The maple leaf was raised and made out of metal, stuck on to the plastic.

"The Canadians used to carve those for girls out of their perspex. Your father gave that to me."

We passed it around, each one rubbing the little raised maple leaf with his or her thumb, before passing it back to Dad.

"Did you love him?" I asked.

She thought for a long time. I liked the way she didn't feel she had to rush in with words to fill the gaps. She had that look about her again as if the rest of us weren't there and she was thinking out loud.

"We thought we loved them all, of course," she said finally. "But did I love your grampa?" She shook her head slightly. "Not really, no. Not the way I loved my Joe."

"He was in love with you," Matt said.

Only Matt could have said that at that moment. She looked right at him.

"Perhaps he was," she said. "But I was married." Long pause. "When it was all over, I was twenty-eight years old...and I had a husband I hadn't seen in six years."

The ash on the second cigarette had got so long

138

and dangly, she just squashed it out.

My mum and I got up to wash the cups and rinse out the teapot. At Mrs. Pigott's request, Dad and Matt looked in the shopping bags and found a fire alarm and some batteries for it. They attached it to the wall beside the glass doors, so she could reach it if she had to without standing on a stool.

When we went back into the living area, Mrs. Anne Pigott, Babe of the Elephant & Shoes, London, England, was sound asleep in her chair.

We made signals to each other to slip away, and we almost had her door closed when Dad turned to us and put his finger to his lips. Then he reached into his pocket and pulled out the photo—the photo of The Babe in front of & Shoes. He stepped back in, leaned over and placed it on the little table by her chair.

We hardly spoke a word on the train ride back to London. And as the fens and channels and old cottages whizzed by outside the window, I don't think I was the only one who looked at them without really seeing them.

And so now there was only one piece of paper left. Mine. My mum took the red pill box out of her pack and removed the, by this time, not-too-sticky bandaids.

"I'll bet Steph wants to balloon across the Serengeti."

"I'll bet she wants to meet someone famous she admires."

"Could we do that?"

"We could try."

My brother unfolded my strip.

"Hunhh? I don't get it," he said.

My mum took it from him, not saying anything, then passed it on to my dad, who nodded slowly.

See, mine was blank.

TWENTY-TWO

As we took off from Heathrow Airport, I looked down at the retreating rows of chimney pots and thought that those buildings were so old they'd have been there when Gramps flew over them years ago. I tried to imagine I was in a Mosquito, looking down. For a split second I saw everything in yellow and brown.

Then a wisp of cloud trailed back from the wing of the 747. Then we were right inside cloud and the ground had disappeared.

It was on the trip home that Matt and I developed our own rhyming slang. A flight attendant is a silver pendant. (You want some pop? Ask the silver.) A magazine is slick and mean. (Hey, skin and blister, hand me that slick.) And it was Matt who figured out why a certain sound emitted from a certain part of the body is referred to as "blowing a raspberry." Raspberry tart rhymes with...

Mum and Dad spent most of the flight talking about how they wanted to live from now on. Dad didn't want to work for a big corporation anymore. He wanted to have a job where he talked about something other than orders and schedules and rising prices. He's taken a job managing a Tim Horton's. (Coffee equals caramel toffee...so he's at the caramel.) He earns a lot less than he used to, but he's good at it, especially the purchasing part, and it means automatic part-time and summer jobs for Matt and me. He likes having all those small interactions in a day, he says, and the fact that no one ever complains about the product.

Mum's working part-time at the bank. They keep trying to ease her up to more than part-time, but so far she's resisted. She's quilting. She took a class to learn how you put the top and bottom together with the batting in the middle, but she absolutely refuses to learn the log cabin pattern or the star or anything like that. She sits down in the basement, just like the woman in Scotland, and stares at pieces of cloth in different arrangements. For her birthday this year Matt and I bought her those knee pads you see in gardening catalogues, and she wears them. Of course, being Mum, she's got her cloth bits arranged by colour and material and stored in plasticized wire baskets or "pollys" (poly gaskets) but that's the extent of her planning. She's learning how to make chaos out of order.

We moved to a smaller house within walking distance of both the bank and the store. We haven't bought a car or a TV. Matt occasionally sleeps outside in the backyard in his sleeping bag. Every now and then I catch him looking at me funny, and he doesn't look away, even after I've caught him.

And me? I'm just waiting. You see, when it comes time to write something on my strip, I want to be able to put something deep and true there. So I'm going through the motions—back to school, parties, movies, Thanksgiving, Halloween, Christmas. Round and round. I even make dinner every seventh day. Why not?

I'm in no hurry. I'm waiting. Because I really did have a headshift. And because once you honestly believe there's no such thing as Tuesday, you never really go back.